WEDDING NIGHT ULTIMATUM

CLARE CONNELLY

Harlequin

PRESENTS

Recycling programs for this product may not exist in your area.

ISBN-13: 978-1-335-21393-8

Wedding Night Ultimatum

Harlequin Enterprises ULC
22 Adelaide St. West, 41st Floor
Toronto, Ontario M5H 4E3, Canada
www.Harlequin.com

HarperCollins Publishers
Macken House, 39/40 Mayor Street Upper,
Dublin 1, D01 C9W8, Ireland
www.HarperCollins.com

Printed in Lithuania

1 2 3 4 5 6 7 8 9 10 LIT 28 27 26 25

Massimiliano was thirty-five years old and in his adult life, he had known many women.

Too many to remember, and none of any particular importance. After his fiancée, all those years ago, he'd made an artform out of sensual, meaningless connections. So much the better if the women he slept with and then walked away from were from noble families. Those same families that had shunned his because of the sins of his father. Those same families that had turned the Moretti name into mud.

But all of those encounters, all of those women, had turned into black shards in his mind, slicing through him accusingly, as he looked down on this beautiful, innocent woman and ached to make her his. No part of him thought he deserved that, and yet, they had a deal. Even without it, Massimiliano knew he didn't have the willpower to resist. Amelia wanted him to be her first, and so help him God, he would be. Just as soon as they were married, and alone...

Clare Connelly was raised in small-town Australia among a family of avid readers. She spent much of her childhood up a tree, Harlequin book in hand. Clare is married to her own real-life hero, and they live in a bungalow near the sea with their two children. She is frequently found staring into space—a surefire sign she is in the world of her characters. She has a penchant for French food and ice-cold champagne, and Harlequin novels continue to be her favorite-ever books. Writing for Harlequin Presents is a long-held dream. Clare can be contacted via clareconnelly.com or on her Facebook page.

Books by Clare Connelly

Harlequin Presents

Pregnant Before the Proposal
Unwanted Royal Wife
Billion-Dollar Secret Between Them
Blackmail to White Veil
Greek's Ring of Redemption

The Diamond Club

His Runaway Royal

Royally Tempted

Twins for His Majesty

A Greek Inheritance Game

Billion-Dollar Dating Deception
Tycoon's Terms of Engagement

Visit the Author Profile page
at Harlequin.com for more titles.

WEDDING NIGHT ULTIMATUM

PROLOGUE

With news of his grandfather's cancer diagnosis still ringing in his ears, Massimiliano Moretti had wasted no time flying to London and seeking her out. He didn't pause to question the wisdom of his plan. Nor to think through the details of how this would work.

Sixteen years ago, he had succeeded in arresting his family's disastrous financial situation through sheer grit and determination, and then, over the course of several years, had taken what was left of their once great fortune and turned it into the kind of wealth that was impossible to fathom. He was now one of the richest men in the world, and he'd achieved that in part because he had followed his gut. His instincts.

And right now, they were telling him he had little time left to fix things for his grandfather.

While he had more than restored their family's financial health, it was their social standing that the older Moretti obsessed over. Once upon a time, the Moretti family had been considered nobility, admired and respected not just in Italy but across Europe and the world. Until Massimiliano's father had betrayed every single one of their aristocratic friends, stealing from them and then running away to avoid paying for his sins. The shock waves had cut through their entire world, destroying everything.

With his father absent, it had been Massimiliano and his grandfather, Antonio Moretti, who'd been left to bear the brunt of their one-time friends' anger, to be excluded and ostracised, left out in the cold. The damage had been wide-reaching, and Massimiliano's life had been changed in many ways. He'd had to see his grandfather shrink in on himself, becoming a shadow of the great, strong man he'd once been. The woman he'd thought he loved had turned her back on him, refusing to have anything to do with the son of a thief. Where Massimiliano had learned to thrive from the challenge presented to him, and grown from the anger of his heartbreak, the older Moretti had been too devastated and destroyed.

Massimiliano had always intended to pave the way back for the Moretti name. Not that he cared at all for such idle concepts as 'honour' and 'bloodlines', particularly after seeing how shallow these people were. Yet, to his grandfather, these concepts mattered.

Which meant Massimiliano was intent on making them happen—and now, with urgency.

He was thirty-five and had not thought of settling down once, since that time when his fiancée dumped him, forced into walking away from Massimiliano because of his father's sins.

He no longer believed in something as antiquated as marriage. And yet, he understood the way these old Italian families worked. So many were crumbling under the financial pressures of maintaining their vast estates, too proud to downsize, too poor to maintain and repair as needed.

Such as the Rossi family, he thought, staring into the small London diner, at the waitress wiping tables. She had fair hair, like starlight, and an ethereally slim build. Her skin was pale and cheeks rosy, classic peaches and cream, undoubtedly from her English father's side. But there was something in the shift of her features, the straightness of her patrician nose, that spoke of her proud family, of the Rossis.

Did she even realise she was practically royalty? That in Italian circles, her family name was spoken with hushed reverence? And did she know her grandparents were on the brink of financial ruin?

Would she care? Enough to fall in line with his plan?

He strode towards the door of the diner, lips pursed in a determined line. He was counting on the fact that she would. Because he intended to marry Amelia Rossi. In making her his bride, his family would once more have something society valued, and his grandfather could rest, when it was his time, in peace.

CHAPTER ONE

THE DOOR SLAMMED shut in the autumnal breeze, and Amelia groaned under her breath. There were ten minutes left before closing and she'd been hoping to make it out on time for once. What were the chances a patron would appear at this late hour?

She pasted a smile on her face at the same time she balled the cloth into her palm, and turned to scan the shabby diner.

But the second her eyes landed on the man just inside the door, every cell in her body seemed to jolt into hectic disarray. He was *nothing* like their usual guest. This man was almost impossible to describe. She'd seen handsome men before. On television, usually, or occasionally in the wild, in the distance, on the Tube, or at a bar, but this man was something else. He wasn't just handsome, he was scorch-your-eyes-out hot, with his tall, broad frame, and dark, swarthy complexion. His hair was thick and a deep brown, almost black, his eyes obsidian, his jaw square, as though it had been sculpted by clay to be as imposing as possible, and his cheekbones were slashed high in his face.

He wore a suit that was definitely not off the high street, and his shoes were polished to a gleam.

She didn't know how long she stood there, staring at him, lips parted, before she collected herself and said, 'Hiya. Can I get you something?'

His dark eyes narrowed, so a shiver ran the length of her spine. Not from fear, but rather because of the electricity that seemed to have dumped itself into the small room.

'You are Amelia Rossi,' he said, disapproval in the deep and accented syllables. She startled at the jarring use of her mother's maiden name.

'Amelia Redgrave,' she corrected automatically, even when she knew it couldn't be a coincidence. Somehow, and for some reason, someone from her mother's past had reached out to her.

One corner of his mouth moved in what was almost a sneer, but he covered it quickly. 'Your mother is Aria Rossi?'

Amelia's heart began to thump. She'd stopped thinking of herself as a Rossi a long time ago, had wilfully turned her back on her Italian heritage, just as her mother had turned her back on Amelia.

'Why are you asking?'

He moved deeper into the diner and, somehow, having his immaculate form in the room made her aware of things she wasn't usually. Like how shabby it was. The flickering fluorescent light above the counter. The faint smell of bleach, from the kitchen.

She refused to feel ashamed, though. Why should she? Amelia had an honest job, and she was working her fingers to the bone at it. Because it felt good to be busy. Good to be distracted. Important not to have too much free time to think about her dad's death after a long battle with cancer, and how empty her life now was.

'Why are you refusing to answer?' he countered, closer still, so she caught a hint of his masculine fragrance over the wafting bleach and her body cried out to inhale again, to breathe in *more* of him.

'Well, for one thing, you're some random guy who's walked in off the street. Why should I answer?'

At that, his lips flickered with something like amusement. It was removed from his face so quickly, she wondered if she'd imagined it.

'Do you serve coffee?'

She blinked at his sudden change in conversation.

'I—yes.'

'I'll take one.'

'To go?'

'I'm in no rush.'

She expelled a soft sigh as she turned away from him. 'How do you have it?' she asked, but her voice shook a little, because the last thing she'd expected was to have a man walk in and ask about her mother. Pain lashed her.

'Black.'

Of course. Why was she not surprised? Everything about this man exuded masculine strength, right down to his coffee choice.

She set about making it but her hands were trembling and she wasn't focused on the job, so twice she had to start from scratch, having made simple mistakes.

'Who are you?' she asked, after a beat, eyes sweeping his face.

'Massimiliano Moretti.'

She stared at him, a solid, stable object in a room that had started to spin. Even Amelia, who'd spent the last several years in a cacophonous whirlwind of brightly lit hospitals, increasingly dingy flats and exhausting jobs, knew who Massimiliano Moretti was. Who wouldn't? One of the richest men in the world, he owned everything from hotel chains to airlincs, shopping malls and sports teams.

The shaking of her fingers was abundantly clear as she lifted the coffee cup and saucer onto the counter and placed them down.

'How do you know my mother?'

'I don't.'

Amelia tamped down on the flash of hope. 'Yet you came here and asked about her.'

'I know her parents.'

Firelight exploded in her belly. Her maternal grandparents were Amelia's last surviving relatives, besides her mother—though she didn't count, as she'd all but died to Amelia when she'd walked out on them. She hadn't thought of her grandparents, though, as family, ever. She didn't know them.

Sometimes, she'd looked in the mirror and tried to pick out the unfamiliar features, the expressions that she'd never seen on her father or mother, and wondered if those belonged to her faraway family, the people she'd never meet.

'Do you know anything about your family, Amelia?'

Her hands formed fists by her side. 'I have no family.' The words were said with ice-cold finality. 'We close in five minutes.'

He continued to stare at her, almost as though he were seeing deep inside her soul, so she turned away and continued packing up the counter.

'Your mother's family is one of the oldest and most respected in Europe.'

She closed her eyes on a wave of feeling. 'I don't want to hear it.'

'It would kill your grandparents to see you like this.'

She whirled around. 'Like what?'

'Working this job, in this place,' he said, gesturing to the diner.

She flinched. 'How dare you sit there and judge me?'

His eyes narrowed. 'I am not judging you, *Contessina*. Calm down. I am stating the facts.'

Contessina. Memories of Aria calling her that speared Amelia's side. She blinked quickly to clear the visceral recollection. 'Yeah, well, we all do what we must, don't we?'

He continued to stare at her in that unnerving way. '*Precisamente*. I'm glad you understand that.'

She frowned. 'I don't follow.'

'You are Amelia Rossi,' he said, so she shook her head.

'I told you; I'm Amelia Redgrave.'

'To the world, you are Amelia Rossi.'

'The world?' she spluttered. 'Who in the world knows or cares about me? No one, Massimiliano.' She stumbled over his multi-syllabic name, making it sound clunky, so he grimaced slightly.

'It's true, no one knows you exist.'

'You knew.'

'*Sì.*'

'Why?'

'Because your grandfather was once a close friend of my grandfather's. When your mother left, and then, when you were born, they discussed it.'

Amelia's heart felt weak at the thought of that. She pressed her back into the full-length fridge, needing support.

'My grandparents know about me?'

His eyes roamed her face. 'Yes.'

Pain lashed her. They knew about her, and had never reached out. She closed her eyes, twisting the key in the lock that kept her Rossi heritage deep down in her chest. Fresh rejection stung.

'So what?' she asked, needing this man to go now. Needing to forget he'd ever been here, stirring up a hornets' nest of her past. 'What is this all about?'

'I think you and I can both give one another something we need.'

She blinked. 'I don't need anything from you.'

He looked at her from head to toe, his gaze raking over her as though she were some object—and an object he found wanting. 'Is that so?'

'What's that supposed to mean?'

'You do not think you could be doing more with your life than this?'

She flinched at his statement, at the accusation contained within. At the dreams she'd long since given up on, because life—reality—the cost of living—had pushed them aside. 'How dare you judge me?' she repeated, shaking her head. 'You have no idea who I am, what I've been through, what this job means to me.'

'I know enough,' he said, voice low and accented.

She stared back at him as realisation bloomed. This was not a stranger. At least, she wasn't a stranger to him. He knew about her. He'd done his research.

'How did you find me?'

His lips shifted in something like admiration. 'It was not difficult.'

'What else did you find out about me?'

His eyes moved with cold determination. 'Everything.'

She closed her own eyes on that, trying to blot him out.

'I know that you're twenty-three years old and drowning in debt, that you lost your father six months ago.'

She blinked back tears.

'Well, you've certainly done your research,' she said, voice uneven. She made her way around the counter, towards the front door. 'And now, we're closing. Please don't worry about paying for your coffee. You need to leave.'

He stood, but, instead of walking towards the door, placed his elbow on the counter, regarding her with a look of indolent interest. 'Would you like to know why I'm here, first?'

Curiosity sparked inside her, but she shook her head. 'I stopped thinking of myself as Italian the day my mother left. Whatever you've come to say, if it has anything to do with her side of the family, I'm not interested.'

'Even when your grandparents are no different from you?'

She stared back at him.

'They were hurt by her, too. You are not the only person she abandoned.'

Amelia closed her eyes against that, a wave of pain washing her from the inside out. 'Please leave.'

'Not until you've heard what I came to say.'

She wanted to argue, but the shock of his arrival, of the things he was bringing up, made her feel weak and light-headed, so she let go of the door and stood there.

Now he moved, stalking towards her and turning the lock, so that they wouldn't be interrupted. She was in too much of a state of shock to argue, or to feel anything like fear.

'You and I have something in common, Amelia,' he said, so close his words whispered across her cheek. She blinked up at him, jolted once more by the perfection of his features. 'We both know what it is like to be abandoned by a parent.'

She frowned.

'My father, when I was nineteen,' he said. 'But first, he scammed every single person we know, stealing hundreds of millions of euros, stashing it offshore, and then, when his criminality was exposed, disappearing without a trace.'

She could only stare up at him.

'My grandfather and I were left to clean up the mess. We were interviewed over and over by the police, who could not believe my father had acted alone. All across Europe, our name—once one of the oldest and most respected—became mud. We were treated with disdain by all we'd once considered friends. In one selfish act, my father destroyed a legacy that had been generations in the making.'

Amelia's curiosity was naturally stirred, and, in truth, she was glad to have something to focus on besides her own family.

'I do not care for legacy, and I would gladly have nothing to do with those two-faced bastards.'

She lifted her brows.

'But my grandfather does care. My grandfather wants, more than anything, to see our family name restored. To be respected once again.'

'You are Massimiliano Moretti,' she pointed out, managing his name with more aplomb the second time around.

'You're worth a gazillion dollars. Surely that buys you respect.'

'Not with these people—they are proud, they are mad, and they are ice cold. Doors remain shut. My grandfather feels that pain daily.'

'I'm sorry,' she said, genuinely. 'But I don't see how I can help.'

'Don't you?' he murmured, eyes tracing her features, as though he was looking for something. 'You are a Rossi. Even from outside, I could tell, just from how you hold yourself. You have your father's complexion, but everything else about you is your mother's.'

She closed her eyes on a wave of fresh hurt. She knew that was true, but, oh, how often she wished it not to be the case. If there had been a way to carefully, surgically remove every single fibre of her mother's DNA from her body, then she would have.

'Did you come here just to insult me?' she asked, voice trembling.

'You know that's not what I intended.'

'Yeah, well, to me…'

'Your mother hurt you,' he said, with a nod. 'But your grandparents did nothing wrong.'

She bit into her lower lip. 'They have never once tried to contact me.'

'You have not contacted them, either.'

'I was a child—'

'You are now a woman.'

'Yeah, well, I've been a little busy lately,' she said, and felt the weight of grief pour over her anew. Nursing her father had been a way of life for so long that she still occasionally forgot he was gone. The reality of how alone she was slammed into her.

'Your grandparents are very proud people, and your family is as ancient as Italy. However, like you, they are in debt.'

She blinked, remembering threads of conversation, of stories she'd been told as a girl. 'My mother's family is wealthy.'

'No. They were, a long time ago. They own property, but much of it is now under mortgage. Their estate is set to be carved up and sold off. It is a situation I have been aware of for some time, though it's only in the last week I have come to fully understand their desperation.'

She couldn't pretend that didn't affect her. She stared up at him, with a heart that had already been so badly hurt by her mother's abandonment, her father's death, and said, beseechingly, 'That's very sad, but I'm in no position to help them. Obviously.'

'I am.'

Her stomach twisted. 'Yes.' She nodded slowly. 'I suppose you are. That's very kind, Mr Moretti.'

'Massimiliano,' he corrected. 'And this is not philanthropy. My help would come at a cost.'

Her brows knitted together. 'I don't understand.'

'After my father left, I swore I would repay everything he took. It almost bankrupted us, and even then, I had to earn more. I took our last million euros and invested it, turning that into two, and then ten, and then a hundred. I do not give money away unless it is an investment; unless there is something in it for me.'

'My grandfather is your grandfather's friend,' she reminded him.

'Friendship is not something I particularly care about—I learned a long time ago it cannot be trusted.'

She flinched at the ruthless certainty in his voice.

'But my grandfather, on the other hand, I would do anything for.'

'Your grandfather,' she repeated.

'I found out, one week ago, that he has cancer.'

Amelia let out a sharp gasp. 'What kind?'

'Why do you ask?'

She lifted one shoulder. 'I've become somewhat of an expert over the last few years,' she said, not telling him the truth. That even before her father's diagnosis, Amelia's deepest held wish was to become a doctor. Ever since she was a little girl, and her best friend had died of leukaemia, she'd been determined to make the world better by helping sick people heal.

'Bladder. We are awaiting tests to see how widespread it is, and what his prognosis will be. His oncologist is not optimistic.'

'I'm so sorry,' she said, genuine sympathy softening the words as tears stung behind her eyes. She knew all about oncologists and prognoses. She had fought, so hard, to get her father the experimental treatment that might have saved his life, but it was prohibitively expensive without an oncologist pushing for him to be in a study, and none had agreed that his prognosis made him a worthy candidate.

'I know he might die. I understand that. But before he does, I would like to give him the one thing he desperately wants. Something my money has never been able to secure for him.'

'Which is?'

'For our family name to be honourable once more. For him to know that his legacy was not destroyed for ever.'

'But, how…?'

'By marrying you, Amelia Rossi. With you as my wife, no one in Italy would think of shunning him. I came here to bring you home—as my bride.'

CHAPTER TWO

AMELIA LAUGHED. She couldn't help it. Though it was nothing like her normal laugh—she'd forgotten what that even sounded like. This was a noise of derision and derangement, a sound that was torn from her against her will.

But seconds passed and the sound died in her throat.

She stared at him, her brain sluggish and slow to cooperate. 'Did you—are you actually serious?'

A muscle throbbed at the base of his jaw, but he simply stared at her, as though that were an answer.

'Why on earth do you think I'd marry you? We literally just met.'

His eyes bored into hers. 'This would not be a normal marriage.'

'Obviously,' she said, rolling her eyes a little. And even though she had no intention of marrying him, her mind began to spin with the idea, picturing herself in this man's orbit, belonging to his world.

It was absurd.

They were chalk and cheese. She was a waitress at a cheap east London diner. He was Massimiliano Moretti. She didn't know how much he was worth, only that he lived in a world of expensive cars and never-ending luxury. She couldn't even cover the interest payments on her credit card. 'And there'll be no marriage.'

He moved infinitesimally closer, so his large frame loomed over hers. 'Even if I could click my fingers and make all of your money problems disappear? If I could do the same for your grandparents?'

Her heart twisted. 'I don't even know them.'

'But you don't want to see them destroyed.'

'Do you?'

'I gave up on feeling loyalty to anyone a long time ago, besides my own grandfather.'

'You said they're friends. Surely he would want you to do something on their behalf.'

His lips shifted in a sneer. 'He would not ask it of me.'

'But—'

'No, Amelia. The only reason I would have for helping your grandparents from financial ruin is if they were family. With you as my wife, I would not feel I had a choice but to intervene.'

Her jaw dropped. 'Are you seriously trying to blackmail me into marriage?'

His eyes narrowed. 'I prefer incentivise.'

'Tomay-to, tomah-to,' she muttered.

'There is your own considerable debt to consider, as well. Not to mention your living circumstances.'

She pulled herself up to her full height. She was not short, and yet he still towered inches over her. 'What's wrong with my living circumstances?'

He ignored the question. 'Is this truly what you want from life, Amelia?' he asked, the words breathing over her, pulling at old wounds, reminding her of the hopes and dreams she'd cherished before her father had become ill and her entire focus had shifted to him.

'Not everyone has the luxury of living their dreams,' she said, the thought one she'd had often. Whenever she caught her mind wandering into 'this isn't fair' territory, and needed to have a stern talking to herself. Because life *wasn't* fair and bemoaning the fact achieved nothing. Far better, in Amelia's opinion, to duck your head and get on with it.

'But you could,' he said. 'Marry me, and you can do and be whatever you want.'

Her jaw dropped as her heart began to race, and, for the first time in she couldn't say how long, something inside her began to lift, giving her a strange kind of hope. Dreams she'd given up on suddenly flared to life once more, tempting her. Tantalising.

But at what cost?

Marriage to a stranger? All so he could trade on a name she'd long ago disavowed. A name she associated with betrayal and hurt, with a side of herself she wished didn't exist. And what would this marriage even look like?

'You could come home, to your grandparents.'

'Italy is not my home.'

'Fine. You could move there for a while, temporarily, and get to know them.'

Her heart turned over and she spun away from him, desperately needing to put physical space between them.

'I don't want to know them,' she said, aware that it was so much more complicated than that. Wanting to know them went hand in hand with not being able to understand why they hadn't ever contacted her. The thought of seeing them brought with it a certainty she would need to take care of herself, for surely they were as cold-hearted as her own mother.

'Are you sure?'

She closed her eyes on a wave of frustration, hating that somehow he was able to see beneath her words, to the truth of her heart.

'I can't marry you,' she said, turning around. 'It goes against everything I believe in.'

'Which is?'

'What do you mean?'

'What is it you believe a marriage should be that makes it so hard to imagine agreeing to my proposal?'

'It's supposed to be a relationship of love, and trust. A couple who want to spend the rest of their lives together.'

His nostrils flared as he expelled a sharp breath. 'That is not what our marriage would be.'

'Obviously.'

'Yet it would still be beneficial, to both of us. Better than the alternative.'

'Are you saying I'm the only person you could possibly marry to fix your family's reputation?'

He stared at her across the diner, features unreadable, eyes dark. 'Your financial situation—and that of your grandparents—makes it more likely you will be reasonable when it comes to negotiating the details of this marriage.'

'You mean, you think you'll have me over a barrel financially, so I'll be more compliant than some fancy society woman with money?'

His eyes glittered, showing the truth of that, and he nodded to confirm it.

'I'm twenty-three,' she said, shaking her head. 'I have my whole life before me.'

'Exactly.' He swept across the diner, minimising the space she'd put between them. 'You have had every disadvantage, Amelia. Life has not been kind to you. So marry me. Become wealthy, and then do whatever the hell you want, without the financial impediments you currently face.'

Her heart twisted. He made it sound so easy. So *good*. But in her experience, there was always a catch.

'Okay, I'll humour you,' she said. She wasn't stupid. While her first instinct was to shut him down, there was no harm in at least hearing him out fully. Her father would encourage her to do that. To get all the details, take some time, then make a decision. She almost heard his voice in her mind, so strong was her certainty that his advice would be thus. 'Tell me exactly how you would imagine this working.' She lifted a hand then. 'I'm not saying yes. I'm just…getting all the facts.'

He nodded, but she could see from the way his body relaxed slightly that he was taking her agreement as a foregone conclusion.

'We would marry quickly. I want my grandfather to have time to enjoy the rewards of this. I can procure a special licence, meaning we'd have the ceremony within a week.'

Her jaw dropped, but she didn't interrupt.

'There would be a financial settlement for you on the day of our wedding—enough to pay off your debt, and make you more comfortable than you can fathom. You would be able to breathe easily for the first time in a long time.' She closed her eyes against the relief of that thought. 'In three months, I would start to clear your grandparents' mortgages.'

'Why three months?' Then, as the penny dropped, 'As an insurance policy against me leaving.'

'Yes.'

'So…this is blackmail.'

At least he didn't correct her to 'incentivising' again.

'How long would you see this "marriage" lasting?'

'As long as my grandfather lives,' he murmured.

'Well, hang on,' she demurred. 'That might be a very long time. You don't know yet. And for your sake, of course, I hope that's the case. I just mean…'

'You don't want to be indefinitely tied to me.'

She nodded once.

'Then let us put a time frame on it. Two years?'

She stared at him, her heart racing. In two years, she'd be twenty-five. 'And then what?'

'We divorce quietly. You would receive, at that point, a large settlement.'

'How large?'

'Large enough that you would never need to work a day in your life. You will never need to worry about paying rent, or buying a single thing.'

She couldn't even imagine what that would be like. Finances had been a struggle for her all her life. Her parents had been broke, and it had got worse after her mother had left. Only, Amelia's goal wasn't to not work. It was to work in the field she was most passionate about. To go to university, study medicine, become a doctor. And with money behind her, she could do that without having to worry about juggling a job at the same time. She could also, depending on how much money he was talking about, help people, like her father, get access to the medications they couldn't currently access. Her eyes lifted to his, trying to see beneath the impenetrable mask of determination. What was this man *actually* like? Just who was she considering making a deal with?

'And our actual marriage?' she asked, looking at him with a face that felt as if it were on fire. 'Would you expect…?' Her voice trailed off and she glanced down at the table.

'No, Amelia. This is not a sexual proposition. *Cristo.* You are far too young for me.'

She glanced up at him sharply. 'Am I?'

'There are twelve years between us,' he pointed out. 'I can barely remember what it was like, being twenty-three.'

She bit into her lip to cover the disappointment that washed over her.

'But we would need to live together. In order for this to work, my grandfather must believe we are genuinely marrying for love. Knowing your grandparents as I do, this would also be the best way to spare them any further pain.'

She blinked across at him.

'They are proud people, Amelia. I expect they will only accept my help if they know it comes from the actions of a man in love.'

'Oh. So we would have to pretend…'

'Yes. Around our families, we would pretend.'

'But behind closed doors?'

'We would live our own lives.'

'In the same house.'

'My apartment is large enough for you to have plenty of privacy.'

Having shared a two-bedroom, one-bathroom flat with three other girls for the last few months, she couldn't even imagine that.

'So we'd be married, but not a couple in any way.'

He dipped his head once.

'And that would be okay with you?'

He arched a brow, silently encouraging her to continue.

'I mean, we just met, but…you don't seem like someone who's not, um…'

'Sexually active?'

She closed her eyes on a wave of embarrassment.

'If I were to see other women, it would be discreet. You would never know.'

She blanched at that.

'And I would expect the same of you.'

Mortification curled around her. What would he say if she told him that she was hardly likely to be running around breaking vows? She hadn't dated in years; not since her father got sick. Before that, she'd shared a few fumbling kisses, nothing more intimate.

'Fine,' she said, dipping her head in acknowledgement.

'It is a simple business proposition, Amelia. Marriage is such a loaded word, because people layer it with emotions and expectations, but if we are clear from the outset as to what we both want, then it is no different from any other contract we might enter into.'

'And would there be a contract?'

He stared at her as though she'd sprouted two heads. 'Of course.'

'I need to think about it,' she said, after a beat. 'How quickly do you need to know?'

'I'm flying to Italy at lunchtime tomorrow. You can either come with me, as my fiancée, or we'll forget I was ever here. It's your decision.' He reached into his pocket and removed a matte grey business card, which he slid across the table. It had his initials, and a phone number.

She ran her finger over the corner of it, looking first at the card and then the man opposite.

'Lunchtime?'

He nodded once. 'Call me any time, if you have other questions.' He turned then, stalking towards the door. 'This is a once-in-a-lifetime opportunity, Amelia. Think of the money, and the ability to connect with your last surviving blood relations.'

He opened the door and turned back to her once more.

'Unless, of course, this—' he gestured to the diner '—is truly enough for you.'

In the diner, he'd worn a suit. Dark charcoal, with a crisp white shirt. So why, when she dreamed of Massimiliano that night, was he wearing nothing whatsoever? Why did her mind so willingly supply an image of him stark naked, approaching her and asking her to marry him? Why did those arms of his—that had done little more than rest at his sides—suddenly wrap around her and drag her against his body? Why did she wake up beaded in sweat, her mind in knots as her body surfed a wave of unfamiliar feelings—of heat and pleasure, of need and wants?

She glanced across the room to see the other bed unoccupied, relieved her room-mate had a penchant for staying out all night. What if Amelia had called out his name in her sleep? Or moaned in response to the dreams that were tormenting her.

She showered early, making herself a pot of tea and sitting at the tiny kitchen counter, staring out at the brick wall opposite, with its colourful graffiti an ever-changing mural for them to admire.

This was hardly the place of her dreams, but it had been all she could afford, after her father's death. It had been hard to hold on, towards the end, but he'd managed to save just enough to help cover rent. And then, he'd slipped from this world, leaving Amelia bereft, alone, and utterly broke. She'd had to move out immediately, and a bed had opened up in this flat-share situation. It was close to work, and the other girls were nice enough. She kept mostly to herself, though. She'd needed to just lick her wounds. She looked around, her heart pounding, to realise that if she were to leave, there would be nothing to take with her. No furniture, no kettle, not even so much as a teacup. She'd sold it all after his death.

This was a once-in-a-lifetime opportunity, as Massimo had said. But she couldn't squander it. He'd made it clear what he wanted, and why. Now it was up to Amelia to consider her wish list, too. Money wasn't enough. Not on its own. He could make all her dreams come true: she just had to be sure to demand it of him.

She was reaching for his card, even before the plan was fully formed, dialling his number and holding her breath as she waited for it to connect.

He couldn't have said with certainty if he'd expected to hear from her or not. While he knew the offer he was making was persuasive—and surely for a woman in her situation, very tempting—there had been such a cool reserve to Amelia. Right up until she'd asked about what their marriage would be like, and her beautiful face had turned bright pink, almost making him laugh at how surprisingly innocent the gesture was.

So when his phone began to ring, early the next morning, and a strange number appeared on his screen, he still didn't think, with any real probability, that it would be her.

'Moretti.'

Then she sucked in a breath and it was somehow so instantly familiar, so like she'd been yesterday, that he gripped the phone tighter.

He wanted this to work.

It was the easiest, most straightforward way to achieve his aim. But it was about more than his family's reputation. While that was at the heart of his plan, he knew that it would bring his grandfather peace, to think Massimiliano had finally settled down, and found love. That he'd met someone he wanted to make a life with. The older Moretti had spoken often of his own marriage, and how happy his life had been. To him, it was the purpose of the work, the money. It was all about family.

For Massimiliano, the opposite was true. He hadn't always been like this, but after his father's betrayal, when the whole world had turned on him, he'd been cut too deeply to recover. Friends had deserted him. His fiancée had walked out on him faster than she could say 'it's over'. He realised how utterly superficial it had all been, and from that point on, he'd known the only relationships he'd ever enter into would be transactional. Easy to walk away from, easy to forget. Comfortingly meaningless.

The women he dated were under no illusions—he

made sure of that. Right from the outset, he laid down the ground rules. There'd been one or two who'd tried to change his mind, who'd thought perhaps he would become attached and want more. But the second Massimiliano thought there was any risk of wanting *more*, he left.

It was his insurance policy, and it had worked brilliantly for him.

But for his grandfather, the constant string of women moving in and out of Massimiliano's life—and bed—was a source of despair. He simply couldn't understand how Massimiliano could live without forming attachments.

'Amelia?'

Another breath sound and then, 'Yes.'

'Have you thought about it?'

'I—have some thoughts, yes,' she murmured. 'Are you free this morning?'

'You don't want to talk over the phone?'

'It's easier in person. I think. Maybe it's not, but it feels—' Another deep breath, this time as though she was steadying herself. 'In person is better. Where can we meet?'

He glanced around his Knightsbridge penthouse, with sweeping views of Hyde Park. 'I'll text you my address, if you'd like to come here?'

There was a beat as she considered that. 'Okay. I'll see you soon.'

CHAPTER THREE

IT WAS MADNESS to be considering this. Madness to have a list of requirements to go through with her prospective fiancé. The man who was all but blackmailing her into a marriage deal.

And yet, he'd been right, the night before. This was her chance to reach out and change her life. Ever since she was a little girl, she'd been in a position of having things happen to her. She couldn't help her parents. The fact their marriage was miserable and they fought often. Nor the fact her mum just simply disappeared one day. That after that they were struggling for every penny they could find. But at least Amelia had been able to apply for a scholarship to study medicine—she'd finally been on her way to the future she'd wanted. Until, that very same week, her dad's cancer had been diagnosed, and she'd known she could never leave him.

These things had happened without her ability to influence them. She'd simply reacted to the circumstances as best she could, behaving, she hoped, in a way she wouldn't regret.

And that same wisdom guided her now.

He was right that, if she let this chance go, she might

very well end up working dead-end jobs for ever, finding it impossible to regain her footing in life.

So why not grab what he was offering with both hands? She'd spent so long looking out for everyone else, including her dad, and becoming an adult way ahead of time, why shouldn't she look after herself for once?

Didn't she deserve to get what she wanted in life?

But there were no compromises here. If she did this, she wanted it to be just what she needed. Which meant being brave, and asking. Demanding. Telling him exactly what would make this worth her while.

Her cheeks flushed pink as she glanced up at the modern-looking building just a stone's throw from Harrods. Two fancily dressed men stood sentinel on either side of the glass doors. She smiled nervously at them as she walked past, then approached the elevators.

She jabbed the button, her stomach in knots as she waited and then, as the elevator began to glide upwards, so fast and smooth, it was unlike anything she'd ever felt. The doors pinged open right onto a huge floor-to-ceiling mirror. She stared across at her reflection. She had set out today in an outfit she usually adored—a simple black pencil skirt and a champagne-coloured camisole, with a denim jacket and high tops. But looking at her reflection, she felt like a misplaced punk rocker in Buckingham Palace.

Closing her eyes as the butterflies in her belly threatened to take up occupation through her entire body, she counted to ten then stepped towards a double set of glossy white timber doors with gold-plated handles.

She lifted her fist and knocked once. It was barely audible. She tried again, louder this time, then jumped back and waited, knotting her fingers as she did so.

He opened the door, and her heart jolted. While he was *not* naked, he wore only a pair of shorts, with a towel wrapped around his neck, dangling on either side of his *very buff,* broad chest, so she could only stare at him, her mouth dry, her blood rushing through her body.

She dragged her gaze, with effort, to his face. 'Were you not expecting me?'

He arched a brow, stepping back and silently inviting her to enter. 'I didn't know how long you'd be.'

She swallowed, trying very hard *not* to breathe in as she passed, because she knew, straight out of the shower like this, he'd smell—*too late.* Her nostrils tingled as she caught a hint of soap and something spicy and alpine. Her gut rolled.

Good Lord, but this man was…too good to be true.

'Coffee?' he asked.

And just like that, he morphed from good to perfection. 'God, yes. Thanks.'

When he walked, he looked as though he'd somehow bottled the power of a thousand lightning bolts and infused them into his body. There was such strength to his movements, such lithe athleticism, that she studied him almost as a work of art. Until she realised she was *still* studying him long after he'd stopped walking, and was simply standing in the kitchen. Looking right at her, his lips quirking with a hint of mocking amusement to find her practically drooling.

Heat flushed her cheeks, but she refused to feel embarrassed. Yet. That might come, given what she intended to ask of him.

'You wanted to talk?' he said, switching on a machine that looked way fancier than the one they had in the diner. She watched as he put freshly ground beans into the basket and lifted it in place, then pushed a button.

'Yeah.' She moved over to the counter and pulled out a seat, sitting down for a second before realising that was wrong, and jumping back to standing.

'You are afraid of me.'

She pulled a face. 'No. I'm…nervous. That's not the same thing.'

'Why?'

'Because I'm tempted to agree with your idea, and that's unhinged. I mean, I can think of a million reasons to say "no".'

'And yet, you're here.'

Her eyes latched to his as all the air whooshed out of her. 'This marriage could make my dreams come true,' she murmured. 'And I gave up on that so long ago. I really never thought I'd have another chance to live the life I wanted, way back, before everything went pear shape.'

'Tell me about that life.'

She sucked in a deep breath, shyness taking hold of her. 'I always wanted more than this.'

His jaw clenched and she wondered if he understood that. How much she'd lost—how much she could have been. 'I've just been getting by for the longest time.' She cleared her throat, not wanting to bore him with the sob story of her life. 'I would love to turn my back on what you're offering, to prove to us both that I'm not that mercenary, but the thing is, I can't. I don't want to, anyway.'

'Do not forget, Amelia, that I approached you. I never offer what I am not willing to pay—and I never give without taking in return. This marriage is important to me, for the sake of my grandfather's pride. In marrying you, I will be giving him something I could never buy.'

'But you will be buying it,' she pointed out, unevenly. 'In a way, you'll be buying me.'

'As I said yesterday, this would be no different from any other business deal.'

She nodded slowly. 'An agreement.' Her voice wobbled. 'That's what I came to talk about.'

'Yes?'

'I don't want to wait until I'm twenty-five to start living my life.'

His eyes narrowed. This man was so imposing, so incredibly intimidating. Was she actually considering marrying him?

'What would you like?'

She sipped her coffee, her hand trembling a little as she placed it back on the counter. 'I want to go to university.' Her brow furrowed. 'I don't speak Italian, but I could apply to study at a British university, online.'

'Why don't you speak Italian?'

She swallowed past the bitterness in her throat. 'Is it a prerequisite?'

His eyes bored into hers. 'You should learn.'

But when she heard Italian, she thought of her mother, and the visceral ache of missing her was so incredibly intense, she almost couldn't bear it. 'I'll think about it.'

He dipped his head once, as if to signal the conversation was closed. 'In terms of university online, I have no issues with that, obviously. I work long hours, and, as I said last night, we will essentially live separate lives. How you keep yourself occupied is of no concern to me.'

She ignored the lump of ice that formed in the middle of her chest at the marriage he was describing. But at the same time, this wasn't a real marriage. She had to get beyond thinking of it as anything like that and focus on it being a trade. A quid pro quo. She had something he needed, and he could substantially change her entire life.

She swallowed. 'There's something else,' she murmured, nervousness tripping through her. But she had no option. Amelia knew she was unlikely to break their vows. While it wasn't a real marriage, she just couldn't bear the thought of being married to one man and dating another, let alone sleeping with them. It went against everything she believed.

'I'm listening.'

He crossed his arms over his chest, with no idea how that was affecting her, making it almost impossible to speak. She took another sip of her coffee. 'I want us to have a wedding night.'

He frowned, perhaps not understanding her at first. But she saw the moment comprehension dawned. 'Why?'

And here she'd been hoping she could just make a demand and have it accepted, without the need to explain. Her cheeks flushed, she moved away from him, towards the windows that showed a view down over Hyde Park. It was easier to talk when she wasn't looking at him.

'I have pretty much no experience with men. I mean, I went to a few parties in high school, had a few fumbling kisses, but nothing amazing. And then my dad got sick. Ever since then, I've been in survival mode. Looking after him, working, trying to pay bills.' Her brow furrowed. 'I haven't had time to even think about meeting someone.' She sucked in a breath, forcing herself to be brave and face him. Turning slowly, she saw he hadn't moved. His body was rigid, his eyes locked to hers.

A frisson ran the length of her spine as she gave herself one last opportunity to back out of this. Not to deliver the counter-proposal that had been running on a loop through her mind since he'd suggested marriage. It wasn't just her inexperience at play, though. There was something about *this* man, the hum she felt in her body when he looked at her, the way the air seemed to crackle as though an electrical storm were stirring to life, that somehow convinced her sex with him would be both eye-opening and satisfying. She dragged in a deep breath and forced herself to be brave. 'I'm a twenty-three-year-old virgin, and if I'm going to get married, I want to have sex with my husband, on our wedding night.'

His jaw was set, his face all angles and darkly assessing eyes. 'You should not barter away your virginity, Amelia.'

'Why not?'

If anything, his response only strengthened her resolve. 'Because your first time should mean something.'

'It will mean something,' she said. 'It will mean I'm doing something for myself. Isn't that enough?'

A muscle flexed low in his jaw. 'Sex will not be part of the bargain.'

'It won't be, after our wedding night. You can go back to whatever it is you do, with whomever you want, and I won't care. This is a one-time proposition.'

'No.'

Her heart flipped. She hadn't expected an instant rejection. It was possible—no, entirely probable—that the way the air crackled between them was one-sided, yet she couldn't give up so easily. She was a fighter, through and through. 'This is a requirement, for me.'

'You're saying if I don't agree to sleep with you, you'll go back to waiting tables, drowning in debt, knowing your grandparents will lose everything they have left that they value?'

She felt the blood drain from her face at his crude summation of her situation. She had no real bargaining strength here. And yet, she did. For all her circumstances were weakened, he wanted something from her. Something that was important enough to him to fly to England and proposition her with a deal worth millions.

'And you'll have to find another woman with the right pedigree who's willing to marry you for the sake of your family's honour, or whatever. A woman who will keep to herself, and have no expectations of you, whatsoever. Or…' she let him digest that a moment '…you can marry me, get everything you want.'

The air between them sparked with her ultimatum.

'This is madness,' he said, with a curt shake of his head. But the words lacked conviction, and she sensed he was on the brink of agreeing.

'Madness is being twenty-three and having no idea what it's like to be touched as a woman.'

A muscle ticced in his jaw as his eyes roamed her face with a different expression now, one of genuine curiosity. 'And you understand that sex is not a precursor to anything more? That sleeping together does not mean anything?'

'Of course,' she almost laughed. 'I'm a virgin, not totally clueless. I get that sex is different from love. And I've already told you, I'm not looking for you to love me.

I know exactly what this marriage is, and if you agree to my terms, then I'm all in.'

Her terms were not exactly onerous. He'd expected her to come with a renewed dollar amount in mind. He'd presumed she'd have googled him, and would know exactly how much he was worth. It would not have surprised him if she'd shown up and asked for a billion dollars in exchange for her hand in marriage. Hell, he'd have paid it.

Coming home with Amelia as his fiancée, the lost daughter of the prestigious Rossis, the sole descendant now of one of Italy's oldest families, would ensure the Moretti name was once more seen to hold value. For his grandfather, he would do anything—even this. It was the final pathway to erase the memory of his father's sins, and the stain it had left on their family's legacy.

But as she stood there, so slim and youthful, with those huge eyes looking at him beseechingly and her fingers fidgeting, he felt a lump of dread forming. This marriage was a business transaction, and he'd have preferred to keep sex out of it altogether. While his would-be wife was beautiful, he could appreciate that academically without needing to take her to bed. There were myriad other women he could seek pleasure with.

Being married to Amelia meant they would be stuck together, in a way he never allowed himself to be with a woman. He couldn't simply walk away when it suited him. Which made it even more important to delineate these boundaries.

He stepped out from behind the counter and moved to her, ignoring the stirring of desire in his gut, the way his body seemed to understand what she was demanding, and was already willing to oblige.

'It would be one night, Amelia. Purely for the sake of meeting your request. It would change nothing about our original deal. I will continue to discreetly date, and I will have no issue with you doing the same.'

Her skin paled ever so slightly but she nodded, her blue eyes sparkling with determination as they met his.

'I told you, I'm not clueless. That's fine by me.'

He held out his hand, to seal the deal as he would any other. But when she put her small, delicate hand in his, his whole body seemed to ignite, so suddenly, their wedding night was almost all he could think of.

Amelia had lived in England her whole life. The only reason she even had a passport was because her father had insisted upon it. *You never know when you might want to grow wings, petal.* Amelia hadn't wanted wings, even when she'd known it had been her father's most deeply held wish. Not when she'd seen what wings could do, the damage they could cause. Her mother had flown away from them without a backwards glance, and from then onwards, Amelia had taken a dim view of the idea of impermanence.

Having lived in England, she had plenty of experience of rain and drizzle but very little of tornados. However, having spent the better part of four hours in the presence of Massimiliano Moretti, she was starting to feel as though she understood what it was like to be caught up in the centre of that kind of phenomenon.

From the minute she'd shaken his hand and agreed to their deal, the wheels had been set in motion. Lawyers were called, a hasty meeting formed to go over the details. All but their wedding night was included in the official documentation, and she understood why he'd omitted that particular component.

She didn't need it in the contracts, anyway. Not when she had his word. Somehow, she just knew he wasn't the kind of man to go back on a deal.

After the lawyers had left, she was sent to the department store down the road to meet with a professional shopper, who spent an hour selecting a complete wardrobe for Amelia as befitted Contessina Amelia Rossi. Everything, from underwear to jeans, suits, dresses, handbags and shoes, was selected and packed away for her. Amelia Redgrave was buried beneath a sea of silk and linen, exquisite tailoring and a colour-matched palette. Make-up was added—everything she could ever need, and from the sorts of brands Amelia always shied away from because a single lip gloss was a week's grocery spend for her. Amelia stared at the accumulating parcels with a sense of dread. She couldn't have hoped to pay for even one of the couture items, let alone the dozens and dozens that were standing in the corner of the personal shopper's office.

'I'll have them sent to the airport, as Signor Moretti requested,' the shopper said with a smile as Amelia walked from the store wearing one of the dresses she'd tried on, in a state of shock, to a waiting car. The luxurious limousine whisked her to the King's Road, where a stunning hair salon welcomed her as though she were the most important client they'd ever seen. Which was saying something, given that there were two very famous actresses in the process of having their tresses seen to.

Amelia, who was naturally blonde, was given a few

extra foils around the front, 'for freshness', the hair stylist had said with a wink, as well as a very skilful cut. While the length was maintained, layers were cut to frame her face and give the hair more wave and bounce. It was blow-dried to take advantage of that, so several voluminous curls formed. While her hair was being done, a manicurist added colour to her fingers and toes.

By the time the manicurist and hairdresser were finished, and the shiny black cape removed, Amelia hardly recognised herself. She reached into her brand-new handbag and removed one of the lipsticks she'd had thrust into her hands by the shopper, and swiped it across her lips. The colour was, as the shopper had promised, the perfect complement to her complexion.

But the face of the woman in the reflection was so polished and expensive. She looked… Her heart sank on the realisation.

She looked like her mother.

Her eyes closed for a moment on a fluttering wave of feelings. Nerves, anxiety and the sense that she wanted to run, as fast and as hard as she could, away from that. Ever since her mother had abandoned them, Amelia had been turning her back on any shared similarities. As a child, she'd been fluent, to an A grade in school level, in both Italian and English, but as soon as Aria had left, Amelia had ceased to speak the language at all, though her father had encouraged her to continue. *I like the way it sounds, pet.*

But to Amelia's ears, it was her mother's language, their shared communication method that had been special and unique, for them.

There was no need to pay for any of the services. When

she pulled a debit card from her new wallet, scrambling to recall just how much she had available, the stylist had shaken her head. 'It's all taken care of, by Signor Moretti.'

Of course it was.

The limousine was waiting at the front of the salon when she stepped out, and, even more conveniently, a takeaway coffee and biscuit were stashed in the centre console.

'Thought you might need a sugar hit,' the driver said, glancing in the rear-view mirror and offering a kindly wink.

She smiled back at him, taking a bite of the biscuit and thinking it was the most normal thing she'd done all day. Despite the fact her stomach was in knots, she chewed on it gratefully as the car slipped through the streets of London, heading north-east, towards the airport.

The whole morning had been a bombardment of appointments, so she hadn't stopped to consider when she would reunite with her fiancé, but now that a new and Cinderella-ified version of herself was en route to the airport, she knew it couldn't be long.

And suddenly, the butterflies that had been kept at bay by how busy and distracted she'd been were ramping up again, hammering her from the inside out. Her eyes tracked the familiar London buildings as the car went past, an affection for this city, her home, clogging her with emotions. But her life here had been far from happy. Even before her mother had left, she could remember their fights. The screaming matches. The worry about money. The certainty that she could never have any of the things her peers did—from dolls to money for sweets. Their flat was cramped, her mother miserable, except for when she put on her favourite music and began to sing, and the whole house suddenly lit up with warmth and love.

The sting of tears caught Amelia by surprise. She blinked quickly, frowning, because she hadn't thought of her mother with anything other than cool detachment in a long time.

Then again, she was going home now. Home to her mother's parents, to her last surviving relatives. Home to reconnect with her Italian side—or at least make peace with it, for as long as she was married.

Buildings gave way to highways and green fields, and then, finally, to the unmistakable hallmarks of an airport terminal. But rather than taking the drive around to the front, the car veered to the right, towards a large security gate with guards on either side. The driver flashed something through his open window, the guards inspected it, nodded, and the gates swept open. Amelia craned forward to see better. It was all so different from her usual world, and she wanted to take in every detail.

The limousine came to a stop beside a glass-fronted building, and before she could so much as undo her seat belt, uniformed staff were rushing forward to open her door with a polite, 'Good afternoon, Signorina Rossi. Signor Moretti is aboard your flight. If you'll come this way, we'll process you for travel as quickly as possible.'

And that they did, from a quick check of her passport, to a reverential and discreet security screening, then she was ushered out of the other side of the terminal, into a waiting black minivan, and driven a short distance to a waiting jet.

A private jet.

Unmistakably, given the matte black colour and the writing down the side—MORETTI.

Her heart stammered right up into her throat as she felt the full force of this man's wealth slam into her anew.

She'd never so much as *been* on a plane, and here he owned this enormous one.

Her body seemed to go into autopilot mode, thankfully, as the car door was opened and she managed to step out, onto a roll of carpet that led the way to the stairs and then up onto the plane. Before she could even take stock of her surrounds, a beautiful woman in uniform appeared, thrusting a glass of champagne into Amelia's hand and smiling brightly.

'Signorina Rossi, what a delight it is to have you on board. Signor Moretti is on a call, but has asked you to be settled for take-off, and says he will join you as soon as possible. Let me show you to a seat.'

Amelia could only blink, her brain whirling with that same sense of having been sucked into the very middle of a tornado. She nodded, clutching the champagne flute like a lifeline, as the elegant woman clipped ahead of her down the aisle of what could only be described as some kind of luxurious penthouse plane. Her jaw dropped and it was beyond her control to change that as she took in the wide, creamy leather armchairs arranged as living room furniture might be. Behind them was a partition, and she suspected the plane would go on in this fashion, like some enormous, palatial sky-home.

'It's incredible, isn't it?' the flight attendant murmured, turning and catching Amelia with her mouth open and eyes frantically scrubbing over the details.

Amelia turned to her, nodding once more.

The woman smiled. 'Please, have a seat,' she offered. Amelia took the armchair closest to the aisle, placing her handbag on the seat beside it. 'Lunch will be served once we've reached cruising altitude.'

'Thank you,' she murmured, to the woman's retreating back. It felt like the most surreal dream she could have conjured. This time, the morning before, she'd been preparing for a double shift in the diner. Today? She was on board her fiancé's luxurious jet, about to set off to Italy.

The diner! She gasped, lifting her free hand to her lips, as she remembered she had a job, and people who were counting on her. She reached into her bag and removed her phone, quickly typing out a text to her manager, asking for some time off. She felt incredibly guilty, but this situation had really just exploded in her face. While letting her employer down wasn't ideal, it truly couldn't be helped, in the circumstances. There was no one else to let know. She'd left a note for her flatmates, but her bed rental was on a week-by-week basis. There were no friends. No one close, who'd care she'd left. Emptiness rolled in her belly.

The noise picked up as the engines began to spin and Amelia settled back in the chair, staring out of the porthole window at the airport and beyond it, in the far distance, the city. A nostalgic smile twisted on her lips, but then the plane began to move, taxiing slowly at first and then picking up speed, so any hint of a smile dropped and she felt a rush of panic for the sheer power of this thing.

A minute later, and the plane was launching into the sky, angling upwards, so the unfamiliar sensations gripped Amelia and she almost gasped. She took another drink of her champagne, and then another, until the glass was drained, but it didn't help to ease her panicked nerves. As the plane soared higher, it encountered clouds, and bumped around a little, which Amelia absolutely hated. And she had the strangest, most ridiculous wish that Massimiliano were there.

Not for Massimiliano himself, per se, but because he was someone else, someone who flew often, who would have been able to reassure her that this was normal.

Instead, she was left to endure this on her own, the first of many new experiences this new version of Amelia was to be thrown into. It was what she'd agreed to—there was nothing for it but to sit back and hope. Hope that it would be okay. Hope that *she* would be okay.

But for Amelia, who'd frequently found that life was willing to throw the worst of the worst at her, hope was hard to cling to.

CHAPTER FOUR

THEY'D BEEN IN the air for almost two hours before Massimiliano emerged from the rear of the plane, striding towards Amelia in a pair of suit trousers, and a business shirt that had been unbuttoned a little at the collar, and with sleeves that were pushed up to reveal his tanned forearms. She'd been with him that morning, when she'd brazenly insisted on sex being included in their marriage agreement, but it was still a shock to see him striding down the plane with all the appearance of some kind of god brought to live with the mortals. He was so incredibly handsome, so strong and muscular, that her breath caught in her lungs for a different reason now.

The delicious meal of garlic scampi and rice, served with a crisp white wine and followed with a cheesecake, had long since been cleared away, and she sat now with a fine bone china cup of tea on the table that came out of her chair's armrest.

He took the seat opposite, not bothering to hide the appraising way his eyes roamed her. Then again, he'd done this to her—his purchased bride. With a few calls, and no doubt a small fortune, he'd turned her from a run-down, exhausted waitress in discounted high-street clothes, to a woman who looked, on the surface at least, as though she were born to zip around in a private jet.

He nodded his approval. 'This suits you.'

She sipped her tea, silently wondering if that was true. While she knew she looked polished, she didn't feel entirely like herself. Maybe she wouldn't for the next two years.

'We must almost be there,' she said.

'Yes. Have you been looked after?'

She let out a soft laugh at the question. 'I've been stuffed full to the brim,' she admitted. 'Your staff is lovely.'

'I'll take your word for it.'

She found it hard to believe a man like Massimiliano hadn't noticed how beautifully elegant his flight attendant was.

'And this is some plane.'

He looked around, as if seeing it through her eyes. 'Yes, it is.'

'I mean, it's enormous, Massimiliano.'

His gaze returned to her face. 'It's necessary.'

She was about to ask him *why*, when he swiftly changed the subject. 'When we get to Rome, you'll be taken to the hotel where you'll be staying for the next week.'

Her insides twisted. She'd spent the whole morning being prodded and primped at his command, and now here he was, laying down yet more orders for her? Where was her free will? Where was her input into this plan?

'Funny, I don't remember us discussing a hotel.'

His eyes narrowed imperceptibly. 'Do you have a better suggestion?'

She realised, too late, that the only alternative was to

stay with him. And for all she'd negotiated a wedding night into their marriage, the idea of spending a week rattling around in whatever luxurious palace he called home had her nerves stretching to breaking point.

'No,' she said, meekly.

He nodded once, moving on. 'Your grandparents are eager to see you. We will have dinner with them, tonight—'

'Wait a second.' The air rushed out of her lungs. 'You've *told* them about this?'

He stared back at her for a beat. 'You know the reason for this marriage, yes?'

She could hardly hear him over the rushing of her blood. She'd signed a contract hours earlier, with six suited lawyers in the room overseeing matters. She *knew* this was going to happen. But somehow, the involvement of her mother's parents made it all feel so unbearably real.

'So, tonight, we dine with your grandparents. Tomorrow night, my grandfather.'

Her heart turned over in her chest at the way his voice deepened slightly.

'And the wedding?'

'Will take place in a week.'

Her jaw dropped.

'The licence is in the process of being procured. The ceremony will be intimate—just us, your grandparents and my grandfather, unless there's anyone else you'd like to invite?'

She shook her head. Even if she'd had close friends, she wouldn't want to involve them in this farce. 'I thought you needed the whole world to know you were marrying me?'

'They will know. I have a PR team engaged to manage that side of things.'

She blinked across at him, with a growing sense that this was ballooning so far out of her comfort zone. 'What exactly will that involve?'

'They'll drop a press release, field enquiries from the media, arrange events for us to attend as necessary, organise interviews.' His eyes glittered with a determination that struck her as utterly unrelenting. He looked as though there was nothing and no one who would ever stand in his way. 'By this time next week, the entire world will know that Contessina Rossi has returned to Italy, and that she has married a Moretti.'

Amelia blinked away, but the twisting in her stomach lasted all the way to Rome.

At this point, she really shouldn't have been surprised by the ease with which Massimiliano could organise incredible grandeur and luxury. Yet she still couldn't quite fathom the way he'd secured such a suite for her accommodation, and had it stocked with all of the clothes, accessories and make-up she'd had selected for her that morning. Was it really only that morning? Her mind whirled at that, to think she'd woken up in her tiny shared flat, contemplating the fork in the road she found herself at, and now she was here. So far down one of those forks there was no turning back.

Amelia had rejected her Italian heritage a long time ago, and yet, almost as soon as she entered her suite and glimpsed the world-famous skyline of Rome, the mix of old and ancient, her heart was humming and buzzing with a need to be out there, rather than in here. To walk the streets that her mother, grandparents, and all her forebears, had trod. To breathe the same air and see if it felt like home, in the same way it did when she was running to catch a Tube or walking along the Thames.

For while the penthouse was stunningly beautiful, it was also very untouchable and intimidating. Whereas this city was a living, breathing part of history, a city that existed beyond just buildings and roads, but that had its own soul. She could feel it, even up here, wrapped in luxury, and what she wanted, more than anything, was to be down amongst it.

She changed quickly, slipping into a pair of tailored trousers and a silk blouse. There were a dozen new pairs of shoes—more than she remembered having seen, much less agreed to—and most of them were heels. But thankfully, the shopper had included a pair of leather loafers, which she opted for. They were supple, soft and incredibly comfortable. Her lips pulled to the side as she reflected on how different her life was from Massimiliano's—and that of anyone of his wealth. Her last pair of shoes had been bought well over a year ago and they were vinyl, not leather. She'd practically worn the sole right through but, until they actually fell apart, they were what she'd had to put up with.

Until today.

Pushing thoughts of her marriage agreement, fiancé and grandparents from her mind, she grabbed her new designer handbag and crossed it over her body, setting off from the hotel to explore this wonderful city while she had a chance to do so.

Massimiliano couldn't fault a single part of the operation. Everything had fallen into place, just as he'd planned. Just as his plans always did.

Amelia's acquiescence had been swift and rational, her requests minimal. And her grandparents had been so thrilled at the prospect of a reunion with the granddaughter they'd thought lost to them for ever that they didn't show even a hint of despair at the idea of her marrying a Moretti.

He'd told them his love affair with Amelia had been brief and intense, and that they couldn't imagine living without being married. It had been strange, saying those words, for Massimiliano knew he would never feel that way in reality. But he hadn't needed to feign his pleasure at the prospect of their marriage. Just hearing the joy in his grandfather's voice had made it worthwhile.

He rode the elevator to Amelia's suite with unwavering commitment to this. Even her insistence on a wedding night was nothing more than a minor inconvenience. Sex was definitely not something he wanted to complicate the easy, professional nature of their transactional marriage, but it wasn't as though he had a track record of letting sex complicate anything. As for Amelia, he had to take her at her word that she could have one night with him and not let it turn into more.

He pressed the buzzer to her suite, hand brushing over the ring box in his pocket. It had been the last piece to collect, something he couldn't simply buy from a jeweller in London. This ring had been in the family safe, and he'd needed to go to Rome to collect it.

He pressed the buzzer again, glancing at his watch. He was right on time, which gave them a small window in the hotel before leaving for dinner. Just long enough to present her with the ring, answer any last questions she had, and then leave.

All according to plan, just as he liked it.

Except, when Amelia opened the door a second later, not only was she far from ready—dressed in a hotel-issue robe with her long blonde hair loose around her face—she looked as though she'd been hurt. Fallen? Her cheek was bright red and there was the beginning of a bruise near her eye.

'Amelia?' He didn't wait to be invited in, but rather, stepped straight through the doors so he could look down at her more closely. 'What happened?'

Her lower lip wobbled as she glanced away from him, towards the lounge suite. What colour there had been in her face dropped, turning her ashen and white, except for the injury.

'You're hurt. Did you fall?'

She glanced up at him again, shaking her head. She lifted a trembling hand to touch her cheek and winced.

'Come, sit down,' he muttered, putting an arm around her waist simply to provide support, guiding her to the leather lounge suite. She didn't argue with him, perching on the edge of the sofa and staring at her knees. She didn't speak, and frustration had him crouching in front of her, so they were at eye height. 'What happened?' he asked again.

When she blinked across at him, her eyes were wet with unshed tears. 'I got mugged.'

The words were whispered. It took him a second to hear them, much less process them. Let alone accept that this woman he'd brought to Rome, and left to fend for herself, had been abused on the street.

'I'm so sorry,' she said as a tear rolled down one cheek. 'It was my handbag. They wanted it and I—I couldn't just give it to them. You'd bought it for me and I'd never had anything quite so nice. It was *stupid*. Stupid. My dad always said to hand over anything thieves ask for. Property is just property. But I was so angry they wanted to take it from me, and when I didn't give them the bag, they—'

'Hit you,' he supplied, anger bursting through him. He stood swiftly, looking around the room. There was a mini-bar, but it wouldn't have what he needed. He picked up the phone and dialled down to Reception, ordering a bucket of ice, before returning to her. 'Did you call the police?'

'I was going to, but a shopkeeper told me there wasn't much point. It all happened so quickly, I wouldn't even be able to give a clear description of them.'

'The shopkeeper was wrong,' he said, nostrils flaring. Later, he would ask her for the details of where it happened, and pass it on to his own security team, but this was not the time.

'I feel so violated,' she said. 'And stupid. I wasn't paying attention to anyone, I was looking around, totally lost in my own world.'

'And you should have been able to lose yourself,' he said. 'This is not your fault.'

'But my bag,' she said, lip wobbling again.

He swore under his breath. 'I'll get you another damn bag, Amelia.'

'You already did,' she said, a watery smile breaking through. 'You bought me four, in fact.'

'I'm glad. And if muggers should want each and every one, I expect you to hand them over.'

But guilt was washing over him, because he should have expected at least the possibility of this. While it was impossible for anyone to yet know that she was a Rossi, he'd turned her, unmistakably, into the *contessina* she was. She looked expensive, and he'd left her to wander these unfamiliar streets, not knowing which she should avoid, what to look out for.

The buzzer rang and he strode through the suite, pulling the door inwards. A hotel staff member stood on the other side, but Massimiliano took the ice bucket with a swift nod of thanks then closed the door, stalking into the kitchenette and tipping half of the ice into a tea towel, which he wrapped into a sort of pillow before carrying it back to Amelia. He lifted it to her cheek, watching her face as she winced again.

'Hold this,' he commanded. 'I'll call your grandparents to reschedule dinner.'

'No,' she said, eyes lancing him now, so powder blue and pretty that he found himself just staring at them for a beat. 'I want to meet them. I just need a few minutes.'

'You can't go out like this.'

'You also bought me like a professional-grade makeup kit. I'm pretty sure something in there will be able to deal with this.'

'It's highly likely there will be photographs of us taken tonight. The restaurant is high profile, your grandparents well known, and I'm—'

'I know.' She nodded once. 'I can manage.'

She probably could. There was an impressive steel to this woman, a determination that he couldn't help but admire, particularly given everything she'd been through.

'You are upset,' he said, surprising them both by putting a hand on her knee, as if to underscore that. But it was a mistake. He saw that the second her eyes flared, unmistakably, with something like awareness, and he felt it spark in his fingertips then travel the length of his body. He pulled his hand away quickly.

'I am upset, yes, but I think the distraction of meeting my grandparents will probably be good for me.'

'You are sure you feel well enough?'

'I'd tell you if not.' She smiled, but it quickly turned into a grimace as the gesture clearly pained her.

'Amelia,' he warned, voice deep.

'I'm *fine*,' she insisted. 'Just…ten minutes.' She stood, and moved through the suite. She looked so incredibly vulnerable in that robe, so petite, that it was little wonder every single one of his protective instincts had burst to life.

He texted his assistant, Tania, as he waited, asking for his security detail to be put on alert that he'd want to speak to them later that night, and also asking her to inform Amelia's grandparents that they were a little behind schedule. And then he waited, staring at the view, in an attempt to blot the image that had scored itself into his brain of Amelia's damaged face—and the knowledge that, somehow, it had been his fault.

True to her word, Amelia stepped out of the bathroom—which was larger than her entire apartment had been in London—nine minutes later, a completely different woman. She'd chosen a stunning shimmery silk skirt and black halter-neck top that tied in a bow at her throat, and to complement the complexity of the neckline had bundled her hair into an elegant bun.

Her make-up had taken the longest, but the kit she'd been provided with was exceptional. There was primer, concealer, both liquid and powder foundation and a setting spray. She moved as quickly as she could to remove the redness and bruising, and then softened the effect with some shimmering bronzer, a sweep of mascara and lipstick. When she stood back to study the work, she was pleased. But nothing compared to the expression on Massimiliano's face when she stepped into the lounge room and his eyes raked over her, his lips parted on a look of obvious surprise.

She'd snapped a pair of black heels in place at the last minute, and they brought her much closer to his height, as well as giving her body a feminine proportion that was so often lacking in her work gear and flats.

'You look almost perfect,' he said, walking towards her without breaking the grip his eyes had on her.

'Almost?' She resisted the urge to pout. 'I have to tell you, I think it's the best I can do.'

'This is not for you to do, but rather me.'

She blinked up at him, not following.

'This is for you to wear, Amelia,' he said, removing a ring box and staring at it for a beat, before cracking it open and turning it so she could see inside. 'It's known as the Moretti diamond, and has been in my family for generations.' He slid the ring onto her finger, and Amelia was glad. She wasn't sure she could have made her hands work well enough to put it on herself.

The ring was *stunning*. A canary yellow diamond solitaire that was easily as large as her thumbnail, set in a high four-claw yellow-gold setting. It sparkled as though it were backlit by a thousand lights, showcasing the purity and perfection of the gem.

'I can't possibly wear this,' she said.

'You must.'

She shook her head. 'Especially not after today. What if someone tries to steal it from me?'

'Believe me, I will make sure nothing like that ever happens to you again.'

A shiver ran down her spine at the cold determination in his voice that almost bordered on violent anger.

'No one will ever touch you against your will, do you understand, Amelia? If I promise you nothing else, let me promise you that.'

Her stomach looped itself into knots, but she *did* believe him. She felt strangely safe, with those words ringing in her ears.

'It's too beautiful. Too old and undoubtedly expensive.' Her eyes lifted to his. 'Right?'

'In truth, it's irreplaceable.'

Now, Amelia's fingers did work. She wrapped them around the ring and removed it, passing it to him as though it were a scalding-hot potato. 'I need something else.'

He frowned.

'A copycat, perhaps, made of glass or cubic zirconia. I don't want to spend the next two years living in a state of permanent fear that I've lost something that valuable.'

'It is special, but it is still just a ring...'

'Not to me, and I don't think to you, or your family, either. Please, save it for your next wife, someone you marry because you're in love, and genuinely want to bring into your family. I can't wear that.'

His expression was shuttered, his lips forming a tight line, as out of nowhere he thought of the first woman he'd intended to marry—with a sense, as always, of betrayal. 'As far as I am concerned, you are the only wife I will ever have, but if you truly cannot bring yourself to wear the ring, I will have another made for you, instead.'

She breathed out a slow sigh of relief. Not only because he was going to replace the ring with something far less valuable, but because he was showing himself to be reasonable, and the more signs she had of that, the more comfortable she became with what she'd agreed to do.

'Will you at least wear it for tonight, though?' he asked, right when she'd thought the matter was closed. 'I will stay by your side the entire time.'

She wanted to argue, because just the thought of having that thing on her finger for several hours was intensely stressful, but, at the same time, she knew why he was asking it of her. If there were pictures of her wearing the Moretti diamond, it would immediately convey what they ostensibly meant to each other. It was all part of the ruse she'd agreed to. The faster it became known that Contessina Rossi was marrying Massimiliano Moretti, the better.

'Okay. Just until there's a cheap replacement,' she murmured. 'And only when you're around.'

CHAPTER FIVE

HE SPENT THE entire drive through Rome asking her questions about the mugging, and between mentally reliving those few scary minutes of her life, and the stunning view beyond their windows, she was almost distracted enough not to be so incredibly aware of the man she'd agreed to marry. The man with his handsome, angular face, broad, powerful chest, and voice that sounded like whisky, gravel and smoke, all at once.

A man who was looking at her with obsidian eyes and that now-familiar determination.

She tried to keep her voice level as she answered his questions, but sitting in the plush limousine with his knee coming within centimetres of brushing her own when they went over a small bump in the road, she found herself wishing for more bumps, and a definite brush.

It was hardly surprising that she should be so aware of him. He was objectively beautiful, and she was almost completely inexperienced. Nothing in her life had prepared her for coming face to face with a man like this, let alone entering into a marriage deal with him.

She trembled as that thought swirled through her mind, and he slipped his phone back in his pocket. 'Tell me about my grandparents,' she said, partly because she wanted to prepare, and partly because she wanted to fill the silence. She was nervous. Nervous to be with this man, to be marrying him, to be knowing that—because of her—that would include sleeping with him, once, as well.

A tension shifted through him, locking his jaw. 'What do you want to know?' he said, after a beat.

'Anything.'

'I have not been in the same room as them for a long time.'

'I thought you said your grandfather is friends with them.'

'Was,' he corrected swiftly. 'Your grandparents were amongst the many people my father cheated. Afterwards, they turned their backs on us.'

Her jaw parted at this new—and relevant—information he'd withheld from her. 'So-o-o-o, they're not likely to be thrilled about this.'

'They are thrilled you are back in Italy. I suspect they will harbour some gratitude to me for having been the mechanism of bringing you here.'

Her eyes swept closed against that. The way it made her sound like an item, rather than a person. The way it neatly skipped over all of her own tumultuous feelings about what being in Italy and back in the bosom of her family meant to her. The betrayal she could feel whispering beneath her skin, at how her father might feel to know that she'd returned to this place, these people, who'd caused him so much grief.

'Oh, God.' She pressed her palm to her stomach as it lurched wildly, her throat constricting with anxiety. 'This is crazy.'

'What is?'

'This. Being here. With you, them. This isn't my life.'

'Your life is nothing to fight for.'

She glared at him then, frustration arcing through her. He was *right*. She knew he was right. She had no family, no friends, no money, and no real prospects. But it was still so new—living in a world without her father. Surely she could be given a period of grace to work things out for herself?

'Can you not do that?'

He held her gaze, silently inviting her to continue.

'Don't sit there surrounded by all your money—and the confidence that brings—and belittle who and what I am.'

He reacted visibly to that, his eyes narrowing and his lips tightening into a hard line. 'It is not you I judge, Amelia. You are barely a woman. The life you lead is not your fault.'

She flinched again. 'Don't you dare blame him.' Damn it. Tears thickened in her throat, and she could only glare at him as she felt the threat of them grow nearer. 'Don't you dare.'

He leaned closer then, surprising her by reaching for her chin to tilt her face his way and hold it there. 'Your mother and your grandparents all had the means to make your life easier. Yet no one lifted a finger for you. But, yes, even your father, may he rest in peace, could have done something.'

'He had no money—'

'I know. But he could have brought you here, Amelia. He could have given *you* a better life. You are a *contessina*, a Rossi—'

'Please,' she groaned, squeezing her eyes shut. 'Look at me. I'm neither of those things.'

But she'd temporarily forgotten the makeover, and the way he'd turned her into some kind of glamorous heiress. 'I am looking.'

'But this is just superficial. It's what you turned me into with a click of your fingers and I can't even think how much money. It's not who I am in here.' She dug her fingers between her breasts, pointing to her heart, but his eyes dropped to the gesture and her breath snagged in her throat. Because they were *close*. His fingers on her chin, her hand between her breasts. And yes, her knee now brushing his, as she'd been hoping it would the entire car trip. Her eyes fluttered closed as a whole host of new feelings overtook her then, making it hard to remember what they'd been arguing about. It was as though his body had turned into some kind of black hole, and she were being sucked inside. When she opened her eyes and blinked up at him, it was impossible to know if he felt it too. If he felt anything.

A moment later, he dropped his hand and settled deeper into his seat, staring straight ahead.

'Your grandmother is Nicoletta and your grandfather Gianni. They live in a large villa, on the outskirts of Rome, and have done for as long as I've known them. I believe Gianni grew up there. They collect art, and antiques. They've been selling off their collection for years, though.'

But she was still in the black hole, sinking deeper and deeper into the fabric of the universe, so his words seemed to come from a thousand miles away.

'Did you know my mother?'

He glanced across at her then. 'Yes.'

Amelia's heart sank to her toes. 'Well?'

'No. She's older than I am. At least ten years, I think. But I saw her, at parties, dinners, that kind of thing.'

A question bubbled in Amelia's chest, but she refused to ask it. She wouldn't give her mother the brain space. And yet it was hard to keep the question 'what was she like?' locked inside her, when she was sitting in the car with a man who probably had more useful memories of her own mother than she did.

'Oh, my goodness.' The svelte Italian woman, who looked to be in her sixties, crossed her chest as Amelia and Massimiliano entered the exclusive restaurant and weaved towards their table. Unlike Amelia, Nicoletta Rossi was tall, but they shared the same slender proportions and fair hair. Amelia had always imagined her grandmother— whenever she'd thought of her—to be a brunette, like her mother. But that must have come from her grandfather, also in his sixties, who still had a thick head of jet-black hair, albeit with a small amount of silver at the temples.

'Amelia,' he said, shaking his head, as if he couldn't believe it was her.

Nervousness spread through Amelia as she hung back a little, as if there were an invisible barrier preventing her from getting closer to the table. As though they were opposing magnetic fields.

Massimiliano turned to her, his eyes probing, as he reached down and laced his fingers through hers, squeezing her hand as he leaned down and whispered, 'It will be over soon. But for now, remember, we are in love.'

Her heart twisted. Loneliness splintered through her like shards of ice, but she nodded quickly and forced a smile to her made-up face. It hurt. She hated to think what the bruise on her cheek would be like the next day.

'Massimiliano.' Gianni's gaze lifted to Massimiliano's. 'You've grown.'

She felt Massimiliano's whole body tense, including the hand that held hers. 'It's been sixteen years,' he pointed out.

'Yes.' The older man's expression was inscrutable as his gaze dropped once more to Amelia. 'Amelia,' he whispered, moving closer. Where Amelia might have taken a step backwards, Massimiliano shifted her way, bringing their bodies close together, as though he sensed she needed that support. 'You are so like your mother and grandmother. It is remarkable.'

She wanted to tell him he wouldn't be so surprised if he'd made any effort to be in her life before this. If he'd so much as called, or sent an email. But she didn't. She hadn't come here to argue with her grandparents. Besides, Massimiliano was right. They'd been hurt by her mother, too. What was this if not a chance for a fresh start? It didn't mean she had to like them, or ever love them, or even have much to do with them. But they were family and, right now, that was important to Amelia.

'Gianni,' she said, holding her hand out to shake, even when she could tell the older man was moving in for a more affectionate embrace. She wasn't ready for that, yet.

He hesitated a moment before shaking her hand, his eyes glancing down and noticing the ring she wore on her other hand.

'The diamond,' he said, looking to his wife. 'So it's true.'

'Yes,' Amelia said with a nod. 'We're getting married.'

'Oh, darling girl.' Nicoletta's eyes were leaking tears. 'You have no idea how I've longed for this.'

Longed for, and done nothing, Amelia thought with a flicker of impatience. But she smothered it, nodding instead, shaking her grandmother's hand. It was hardly the warmth and joy they might have been hoping for, but Amelia was here. And so, thankfully, was Massimiliano, because without him, she wasn't sure she could have got through the evening with anything like aplomb. But despite the fact he'd exuded a cool, single-minded determination ever since they'd met, in this environment, she saw a different facet. He spoke easily with her grandparents, about subjects they had in common—art investments, his hotels—so Amelia found herself sitting there feeling like a child at the grown-ups' table. By the time coffee was served, it was a relief to know the night was almost over.

Massimiliano had also relaxed into the role of fiancé. His arm was stretched along the back of Amelia's chair, his fingers dangling carelessly across her shoulder, so sparks flew through her body, making it almost impossible to think straight.

'Tell us about the wedding,' Nicoletta invited, leaving Amelia totally tongue-tied. Because of course she knew none of the specifics, and she cursed herself then for not having asked more questions.

'It will be Saturday morning,' Massimiliano answered, naming a church with a long Italian name. 'I presume you can make it?'

'Make it,' Nicoletta sobbed. 'We wouldn't miss it for the world. We never got—' She closed her eyes then, on a wave of emotion, and Amelia understood. They'd never seen their own daughter's wedding, as Amelia's parents had eloped. 'We wouldn't miss it,' she repeated.

'Shall we send you a guest list?' Gianni suggested. 'I know many of our friends would like to see—'

'No.' For a moment, Massimiliano's mask of congeniality dropped. 'It will just be the five of us.'

'Five?'

'My grandfather.'

At that, Gianni's face paled. 'I see.'

Amelia glanced at her future husband and saw the glint in his eyes, the muscle throbbing in his jaw, and realised she wasn't the only one riding a wave of difficult emotions. She put her hand out instinctively, curving it over his thigh, to bring him back to the moment. The pretence. But touching him was like setting off a whole bundle of fireworks, just beneath her skin, so she gasped softly, drawing his gaze to her face. Her parted lips. And dropping his head, before she could realise what he intended, suddenly, he was kissing her.

The whole world tilted.

Then shot into Technicolor.

Then seemed to explode with a heat and sparks, until she could hardly think straight. It was over too quickly. Just a brush of his lips against hers, no doubt for her grandparents' sake, but if she'd thought touching his legs had set off fireworks, then the promise of a real kiss, at some other point, had her tingling from head to toe. She couldn't look away from him, and, for a moment, she wondered if the same was true for him, as his eyes held to hers, boring through her with the force of his gaze.

'You'll send us all the details,' Nicoletta murmured, all but slicing through the moment like a knife.

Sure enough, Massimiliano shifted, moving his leg beneath the table so her hand dropped free, but thankfully leaving his own fingers still trailing on her exposed shoulder. 'Of course,' he said. 'My assistant will be in touch. Naturally, I'll send a car to collect you.'

'That's not necessary.'

'It's our wedding. Of course I shall take care of the details.'

Gianni nodded, clearly sensing there was no point arguing with Massimiliano. 'Very well.'

With a few more pleasantries exchanged, the dinner was over. As they slid back into the limousine, Amelia expelled a long, slow sigh, closing her eyes as she tried to process everything that had just happened.

'Was it as bad as you thought?' he asked and, with her eyes closed, his voice wrapped around her like silk.

'Better in some ways, worse in others.'

He made a grunting sound, which she took to be of agreement.

'You don't like them, do you?' she asked, softly.

'Why do you say that?'

She pulled a face. 'I have eyes and ears.'

He let out a short bark of something like laughter as the car pulled into traffic. 'I take a dim view of people like them. It's not personal.'

'Isn't it?' she murmured. 'It sounds like the people you cared for let you down the most.'

'They were my grandfather's friends, not mine.'

'Still, it must have hurt you to see him hurt.'

'Every single person we once thought of as a friend turned their backs on us. People I would never have thought capable of it. Overnight, the name Moretti became a joke.' His eyes glittered when they locked to hers. 'It still would be, were it not for my net worth.'

'And now, me.'

'*Sì*. And now, you.'

A shiver ran the length of her spine as she felt his possessive heat twist around her. But it wasn't about possessing her in the way she now realised she wanted. This had nothing to do with her as a person, or as a woman, and everything to do with the status her name brought.

'And the whole world will soon know about it.'

Her heart sank. She understood bitterness and anger. She would feel it in bucketloads, if she let herself. But the idea of this marriage being born from those things filled her with a slow-spreading sense of dread.

'Why did you kiss me, Massimiliano?' she asked, after several moments of silence. Unbeknownst to her, he'd been asking himself the same question ever since. But she'd looked up at him with those big, pale blue eyes, and softly parted lips, he'd caught a glimpse of the bruising on her cheekbone and had simply acted on instinct. Leaning down, brushing his lips over hers. To comfort and console, to give confidence and calm.

It hadn't worked. Calm had evaded him ever since. Because with that one simple gesture, that one touch, he'd felt yearning ignite in the pit of his belly, and a familiar, aching need pulsing through him. Demanding more. More of this woman he'd negotiated into marriage, more of this woman he hadn't intended to touch, much less look at twice. He'd told himself it was little more than a contractual arrangement, like any other business merger, but he'd never wanted to rip the clothes off any of his other contractual partners, the way he'd been fantasising about doing with Amelia all night.

She shifted, moving closer to him, as if to ask the question again. He tilted his gaze down to hers, knowing he should be honest, but aware that it would be opening a can of worms he didn't particularly wish to deal with. 'Because we were pretending, remember?'

He saw the way her eyes softened, hurt obvious in their depths. It wasn't just that she was younger than him, but that she was so inexperienced. And perhaps that she felt too deeply, couldn't conceal as well as him. Maybe she'd never needed to? Whatever the reason, he saw whatever she was feeling, and really wished he didn't.

Because hurting Amelia didn't have any place in his plans. Yet if he told her that he'd kissed her because she'd looked so hauntingly beautiful, and he'd wanted to kiss her so much harder and deeper than that, would she read more into it than he intended? He wouldn't take that risk. Better to downplay it.

Except his body didn't get the memo, and his hand was moving, slowly, towards her cheek, his fingertips brushing over the flesh that, beneath her make-up, would show the bruising. 'How does this feel?'

'Worse,' she admitted, but her voice was cool, as though she was trying to pull back from him. 'But I'll live.'

He nodded once. 'My security team will be providing bodyguard support to you, going forward.'

She startled visibly. 'What?'

'For when you leave the hotel.'

'No. That's…crazy. I don't need a bodyguard.'

'I should have thought of it before this. No one should ever have been able to touch you.'

'It was just bad luck. I went down the wrong street, wasn't paying attention…'

'And that same bad luck could happen again. So you'll be accompanied either by me, or by one of my team.'

Her jaw dropped. 'I don't think I want a bodyguard.'

'It's not unusual.'

'I beg your pardon, but, for someone like me, it's exactly that.'

'Either you accept the necessity of a bodyguard, or you move in with me immediately. The choice is yours.'

Her jaw dropped. 'That doesn't really sound like a choice, so much as an ultimatum.'

'It's common sense.'

'No, it's bossy, arrogant and demanding. What gives you the right—?'

'This,' he said, moving his other hand to hers and brushing the flesh just beneath the Moretti diamond. 'You are my fiancée—'

'In name only.'

'No, not in name only,' he retorted, surprised by the anger she'd stirred him to, the feelings she'd evoked with this argument. 'To the rest of the world, you are my fiancée, and will soon be my bride. That makes you a very valuable target. Surely you comprehend that?'

He saw the fear tremble across her features and instantly regretted being so frank with her. But he had to make her understand. What had happened on the streets that afternoon had been a random mugging, possibly brought on by the designer bag she was wearing, and the fact she looked like an easy hit because of her diminutive stature. But once word got out that they were married, it was the less random attacks he'd worry about.

'I can take care of myself.'

'Perhaps, and yet, you no longer have to.'

'That's no reason to give up my personal freedom—'

He stifled a scoffing sound. 'Don't be so dramatic. We're talking about highly trained security operatives accompanying you out in public. You will not even know they're there.'

'I'll know.'

It had been a long time since anyone had argued with Massimiliano like this. Most people saw the writing on the wall as soon as he laid down a proposal. He had to admit, sparring with her was equal parts frustrating and addictive.

'Why are you fighting this so hard?'

'I just don't see the point.'

'Even after what you went through today?' Irritation swirled through him, and he attempted to tamp down on it. But it was intense and flooding his system, and for the first time in a long time, he felt a sense of being out of control. 'You are being unreasonable.'

'And you're being overbearing.'

'By wanting to keep you safe?'

'You seem to think you're safe enough and I don't see you being trailed around by discreet security guards.'

His irritation turned into impatience, and something else. A fire in his bloodstream. 'I have security protocols in place.'

'But not bodyguards?'

'I also do not look as though a gentle breeze could knock me down. You, on the other hand, are tiny. Like a doll. It would take no effort to bundle you into a waiting car and kidnap you for ransom. Do you not understand that?'

He saw something flash in her eyes, and wondered if he'd gone too far. If he'd scared her, with that warning. But she rallied quickly, glaring back at him. 'I won't let that happen.'

'You are being so unreasonable,' he growled, moving closer without meaning to, even as alarm bells sounded in his mind.

'By standing up for myself?'

'I'm trying to protect you, damn it,' he retorted. 'You are—just—seriously—'

'Yeah? What am I, Massimiliano?'

How could he answer that? What words would suffice? But even as he was racking his brain for something to say, for a response that was justified, his body was moving the rest of the way, his head dipping, his hand on her chin tilting her face higher, so that when his lips claimed hers, she was right exactly where he needed her to be. And this time, it was so much more than a simple brushing of mouth to mouth. This time, his whole world caught fire before he could stop it.

CHAPTER SIX

Amelia had been kissed before. At least, right up until that moment, she'd *thought* she had. But it took no time whatsoever to realise that nothing and no one in her life had prepared her for the onslaught of this kind of kiss. His lips were masterful and dominating, pressing against her until her lips parted and his tongue could probe inside, duelling with hers, as each movement was like a whip against her flesh, driving her closer to him, so, without her realising it, her hands were clutching his shirt as though her life depended on it.

He was warm and hard, his body like a soldier's, all buff and broad, and his hands were every bit as commanding as his mouth, knowing just where to touch and hold to keep her utterly enslaved to this moment.

Heat built in her belly, then sparked through her entire body. She moaned softly against his mouth, and when he pulled away, she almost cried out at the deprivation. Except he was only relocating, shifting his attention to the skin beneath her earlobe, so she dug her nails into his shoulder and tilted her head back on a wave of fiery ecstasy.

It was better than anything she'd ever known.

And then, it was over.

He was pulling away from her, despite the clutch she had on his shirt, staring down at her with darkly glittering eyes. 'You will have a team of bodyguards, or you will move in with me right now. What's it to be, *cara?'*

She couldn't think, much less speak. His words seemed to be coming from such a long way away, through a fog of confusion. But she did hear the calmness in his voice, the way he sounded utterly normal. Unaffected by what had just happened.

She dropped her hands to her lap, tearing her gaze away to stare down at them. Or, more specifically, the diamond. And it rammed home what should have been perfectly obvious. They hadn't needed to argue about a bodyguard. Obviously it was a wise precaution, and completely normal for people in this *milieu*. Soon, the whole world would know she'd married one of the wealthiest men in existence. Of course that made her vulnerable, just as he'd said. A shiver ran through her, but she nodded once.

'A bodyguard will be fine.' Her own voice sounded clipped to her ears, but at least it didn't emerge small or weak. She forced herself to look back up into his face, then wished she hadn't when she caught the triumph flaring in his eyes.

'Good decision, Amelia.' It was only then she realised he'd called her *cara* earlier, and that she'd liked it. 'Now, let me tuck you in.'

Her eyes flared wide and hope speared her right in the chest, but it was a false hope. After the heat of that kiss, Massimiliano had returned to an almost stranger-like presence. Their walk from the car to the lift was wordless, and then, from the lift to her front door, he simply went through the logistics of the following evening.

'If you feel you cannot come, just send me a text. I can reschedule.'

She frowned. 'Why wouldn't I be able to come?'

His hand lifted then, gently cupping her cheek, his eyes shifting to the same space. Her stomach lurched at the contact—at how much more she wanted. 'If this gets worse.'

'It's fine,' she promised.

'Does it hurt?'

She nodded.

'Do you need anything?'

Her lip curled in a half-smile. 'Do you even need to ask?'

His eyes flared in surprise and then he dropped his hand and took a step back. 'One night, Amelia—and it is not tonight.'

She swallowed past her disappointment, but covered it quickly. 'I'll see you tomorrow.' She swiped her keycard and went to open the door, halfway hoping he'd reach for her and kiss her again, but he didn't. She had to wait until she fell asleep for some more satisfaction on the Massimiliano front.

The kiss had been a godawful mistake. Worse than the brushing of their lips in the restaurant, because now he knew how compatible they were. He'd kissed her and his whole body had lit up like a Christmas tree, responding instantly to her warmth and curiosity, to the way she was so utterly intuitive. Her moans had been like flicks of lava against his skin, heating him all the way through. If she'd been any other woman, there was no way he would have stopped it when he had. Hell, he'd have dragged her into his lap and fucked her then and there, making her scream his name at the top of her lungs, not caring who on the outside pavement heard, not caring about anything in that glorious, heady moment of possession.

But Amelia was not any other woman.

She was inexperienced. Almost completely, going from the way a single kiss had turned her to jelly. Yet she was also incredibly sensual, so he found it impossible to believe she hadn't been with a man. Her desires were so strong, her body's needs impossible to miss. How had curiosity not got the better of her before this? Her father's illness had been protracted, he gathered, but even prior to that? Surely as a teenager, she'd wanted to mess around as hormones gripped her. Young men must have beaten a path to her door, given how beautiful she was.

It didn't matter, though. His task was not to psycho-analyse her, or get to the bottom of her inexperience. It was simply to show her what sex could be. And all of a sudden, there was a rush of power inside his chest, an ancient, archaic instinct of pride that he would be the first man to teach her what her body was capable of. Gratitude as well, because he knew that, with his dying breath, he would make the experience everything it should be for her. He would send her over the edge again, and again, until she almost couldn't bear it. If they only had one night together, he would damn well make it count.

The skin discolouration was worse the next night. So much so, Amelia had to find make-up tutorial videos on the Internet, with instructions for how to cover bruising.

It took her down a rather depressing rabbit hole, but with the information gathered, she set to work, deftly mirroring the make-up artist's ministrations until her face looked normal. No, better than normal, because on top of the foundation base, she'd experimented with contouring, and she had to admit the effect was worth the effort.

She'd never really been hugely into make-up. Whether that was a question of time, or money, or just who she was, she hadn't been like her peers in high school who'd caked their complexions and extended their eyelashes from as soon as they could buy beauty products. She preferred the feeling of not wearing anything on her face except the lightest of cosmetics.

But for the next two years, she wasn't herself. Not really. She was Amelia Rossi, and soon, Amelia Moretti. She would be the woman everyone expected—glamorous, elegant and with the utmost attention paid to her appearance.

She dressed accordingly, choosing a cream trouser suit and teaming it with a vibrant blue camisole that drew focus to the hue of her eyes. Tonight, she wore her hair loose and waved around her face. She'd paid attention when the stylist was working on it in London, and managed to achieve a similar look. Wearing her hair down had the added advantage of being distracting, somehow, from her face—making it even less likely people would notice her cheek.

She was ready several minutes ahead of the time Massimiliano had stipulated, unlike the night before, when shock had made her completely lose track of everything. It had been so much better that way, though. Now, all dressed up, and waiting for the doorbell, she felt her nerves build and build, replay last night's kiss, every touch, until her insides were trembling with the force of her anticipation.

Which was really stupid.

His parting shot, the night before, had been to remind her that their wedding night would be the one and only chance for them to sleep together—per his contractual obligation. It wasn't going to happen beforehand.

But why had he kissed her a second time? In the restaurant, she could understand. That kiss had been chaste, and for the benefit of her grandparents. But in the limousine, with no one to bear witness, it had just been about him, and her. And it had been so sensual, so incredibly hot, that a host of unfamiliar feelings had scuttled her brain power completely. She would have done anything he'd asked of her in that moment. Anything.

It both terrified and empowered her. She felt as though she was on the brink of something vital, something that would give her answers she'd wanted for a long time, and hadn't known to reach for.

She felt as though she was stepping into her feminine power, and it was all because of this stranger, really—for that was what he was. And better for him to stay that way. After the power of the kiss the night before, she'd realised that someone like her—inexperienced and ill-equipped to deal with a man such as Massimiliano—could absolutely mistake the incredible rushing of sensual heat for something else. And the last thing she wanted to do was develop a crush on her husband.

Particularly when he had been so clear about what this relationship was, and always would be to him.

He'd even stipulated that he would continue seeing

other women! For all she knew, he had plans to see them this week, in the lead-up to their wedding. After all, why wouldn't he? It wasn't as though a simple kiss in the back of a limousine were enough to derail his life, and none of this was personal to him. Not in the relationship sense, anyway. This was all about her name, her mother's name, the heritage she'd shunned, almost her entire life.

Anticipation and warmth fizzled out, to be replaced by cold dispassion. Pain from the past had long fingers, and they were wrapping their ice-like bones around her now, so she paled perceptibly. Rubbing her hands together, she paced the suite, wishing she could do something to stem that pain.

But meeting her grandparents had brought it all back to the surface. The way they'd stared at her, as though she were their daughter, finally returned to them. As though…as though she were everything they'd been waiting for. When the truth was, they hadn't ever bothered to try contacting her. Did they have any idea what that would have meant to Amelia? To know that, while her mother had abandoned her, there were people, besides her father, who wanted her in their lives?

She was still pacing when, a moment later, the buzzer for her suite sounded and her heart kicked up a gear. Thoughts of her grandparents were totally scattered from her mind, replaced by memories of last night. That kiss they'd shared. The heat that had spread through her. The way she'd felt as though he were the only person on earth.

Her pulse surged like a tsunami inside her as she moved quickly towards the door and pulled it inwards, her breath hitching in her throat as she stared out at the man opposite. He wore a dark grey suit, a pale blue shirt, and looked good enough to eat. Heat flushed her cheeks and her knees felt weak.

'Hi,' she said, noticing the way his eyes swept over her body first before landing on her cheek as a frown etched across his face.

'How does it feel?'

She lifted one shoulder. 'It's okay. Looks worse, feels a bit better. It was hard to sleep, though. Every time I rolled onto that side, I woke up.'

She was sure she wasn't imagining the way his eyes flared in response to that. The image of her in bed?

'Did you want to come in?'

'No.' His answer came out quickly. He seemed to want to soften that with a smile, but it appeared more of a grimace. 'We should go. Are you ready?'

She glanced down at her outfit with a nod. 'I just need my bag. I won't be long.'

'And your ring,' he reminded her.

She shot him a look. 'You're sure?'

'Until your replacement arrives, *assolutamente*.'

She bit into her lip. She felt a hint of compunction at having him order a cheap dupe, but it was better than wearing something so priceless and irreplaceable.

She disappeared back into the hotel suite, scooped up her clutch bag, slid the diamond ring in place, then returned to the door, where he was waiting.

'Let's go,' she murmured, ignoring the way her insides were trembling.

The elevator was a form of agony. Being so close to him, in an enclosed space, she couldn't help but be intimately aware of his entire body, nor to focus on how much she wanted him to reach out and pull her into his arms, to kiss her as he had in the car that night. He didn't. They swooped to ground level, walked side by side across the lobby, and then they were back in his limousine.

Amelia sat with her hands clasped in her lap and back ramrod straight the whole way there. Every shift he made, every movement, made her aware of him in a way that was making her lose her mind. Tension zipped through her and desire flared in the pit of her stomach.

Meeting his grandfather was important, but, in that moment, she desperately prayed for the car to break down. Something that would strand them together in an enclosed space, so that he might kiss her all over again.

Of course, there was no such luck. His expensive car was meticulously maintained, and it purred and hummed all the way across Rome. She was not remotely familiar with the city, but all metropolises shared certain hallmarks. She knew, for instance, that the buildings had become smaller, the graffiti more prominent, the cars parked on either side less expensive and modern. The car finally drew to a stop outside an unassuming, warmly lit trattoria with green and white striped awnings and small, round tables for two lined up on the footpath.

'What is this place?' she asked, instantly captivated.

'You don't approve?'

'Are you kidding? It kind of reminds me of the diner.'

He let out a laugh. 'In what way?'

'It looks welcoming. No airs and graces.'

'It also has, in my opinion, the best food in the entire city.'

She turned to face him, and instantly wished she hadn't. He'd leaned closer to her, to see out of her window, so, with that one simple movement, she was looking right at his profile. Her throat constricted as her gaze roamed his angular cheekbones then dropped to his stubble-covered jaw, and finally settled on his mouth. That magical, insanely addictive mouth…

He turned slowly, as if he was aware of the risks in that. That in one simple movement, he could bring them back together again.

Her lips parted on a rush of breath and her heart stammered against her ribs. She moved forward infinitesimally, the need for his touch overtaking every other emotion. 'Massimiliano,' she murmured, lifting a hand to his chest. Their eyes locked and she felt a surge of desire, a suffocating need, and she was pretty sure he felt it too, going by the way his gaze dropped to her lips and lingered there.

His hand lifted though, his thumb padding across her pink lips, pulling the lower to the side. 'One night, Amelia. And not tonight.'

It was almost verbatim what he'd said when he'd dropped her home the night before.

Maybe she was wrong about his desiring her. Or perhaps he was just way better at controlling his instincts. It was hard not to take it personally, though, when her whole body seemed to catch fire if he was nearby.

Before she could say anything in response, her door was being opened by the driver, and Massimiliano was moving towards his own side, to get out of the car.

She watched him a moment, frowning, before pulling herself together and stepping onto the footpath, careful not to lose her footing in the sky-high heels.

A moment later, he was by her side, arm weaving around her waist, drawing her to him, so those fires that had been lit the moment he'd arrived at the hotel went into full-blown explosives territory.

'Show time.'

Her heart turned over in her chest.

Yes, it was show time. A game of pretend. Nothing about this was real. Except for her reactions to him…

'I'm ready,' she said, forcing an over-bright smile as she glanced up at his face. His features were locked carefully into place, a mask of determination, and then they were walking forwards, together, towards the unassuming little restaurant. There were no suited staff here, so it was Massimiliano who stepped forward and pushed the door inwards, holding it for her, before returning his hand to her waist.

Inside was so much sweeter than she'd expected. Red and white tablecloths covered each sturdy timber table, the chairs were black bentwood, the lighting was warm and casual, there were ferns in pots dotted around to create a pleasing effect and old Chianti bottles had been pushed into service as makeshift candle holders on each table, their round bodies rumpled by wax pillars. The air was heavy with the fragrance of garlic and herbs, and in the corner there was a rustic-looking brick pizza oven, very clearly in use.

'It's wonderful,' she murmured, smiling.

When she glanced up at Massimiliano, there was something in his face that made her insides go all warm and soft. Approval. Appreciation. It was gone again almost as quickly, but she was sure she'd seen it.

Amelia cleared her throat, eyes scanning the restaurant for people now. It was busy, though, unlike the place they'd gone the night before, this trattoria was filled with families, elderly couples, there was a group of female friends sharing a bottle of red wine and pizzas. There was a lot of ambient noise—chatter and laughter, and also, the gentle strains of Italian singing coming from crackly speakers in the corners of the ceiling.

'Is there anything I need to know about your grandfather?' she asked, realising it was probably a question she should have asked in the car.

'Such as?'

'Other than what I already know.'

He stopped walking and looked down on her. 'He's one of the best people you will ever meet. Honourable, intelligent and proud. I think you'll like him.'

'Is he…' she hesitated, not wanting to be insensitive '…unwell?'

'No. His cancer was detected in a routine check-up. So far, he has no symptoms, beyond a little exhaustion. He'll start treatment this week.'

Panic squeezed her throat. A muscle memory, rather than related to anything he'd said. But she'd spent so long advocating for her father to have the benefit of the experimental drugs that were showing such promise, and without success. She would have put money on that not being an issue for Massimiliano's grandfather. Despite his age, and no matter his prognosis, money talked, and that he had in abundance. The bitterness she felt had nothing to do with resenting Massimiliano's ability to fund that medical care. It was fuelled by injustice—of cancer in general, and the practicalities of treatment.

'Ready?' he prompted, lifting his gaze and scanning the restaurant.

'Of course. Let's do this.'

His hand shifted to the small of her back, fingers splayed wide, so she felt his presence in her whole body. Arrows of desire needled just beneath her skin as they weaved through the restaurant, towards a table at the back.

The moment Amelia saw Massimiliano's grandfather, she was struck by the similarities. Far from appearing like someone who was facing cancer, he looked to be the picture of health and vitality. Knowing Massimiliano's age, she figured his grandfather had to be in his seventies, at least, yet he was clearly in great shape. He wore a light grey suit and polished brown shoes, and his hair, once the colour of Massimiliano's, she guessed, was now a slate grey.

'Massi,' he said, shaking Massimiliano's hand before pulling him into an embrace, slapping his back.

'*Nonno.*' Massimiliano surprised her by using the affectionate title for Grandpa. He pulled away from the older man and gestured to Amelia. 'This is Amelia Rossi.'

Antonio stepped forward, intelligent dark eyes locking to her thoughtfully. 'So it is,' he agreed, nodding slowly, his face lined in a way she hadn't seen at first. Unlike his grandson, Antonio's smile came easily. 'I knew your mother, once upon a time. And your grandparents.'

'Massimiliano's mentioned that.'

'Of course he has.' He shook his head. 'I'm a little thrown. You are so much more like her than I expected.'

Amelia winced, and she knew Massimiliano noticed the response, because his hand, in her back, began to brush over her spine, as if to bring her back to the moment, or perhaps even to offer comfort. 'So I've been told,' she managed to respond, her voice carefully blanked of emotion. Inside, though, she ran from the words, from what people might have thought of as a compliment.

'You do not agree?'

'I haven't seen my mother in a long time.'

Antonio's eyes flicked to Massimiliano's, his expression showing confusion, and then embarrassment. As though he'd said something wrong.

'You weren't to know,' she murmured, reaching out to put a hand on his. 'My mother…left, my father and me, when I was just a girl. I haven't seen her since.'

Antonio's surprise was evident. She wondered why Massimiliano hadn't told his grandfather. Then again, this had all happened so quickly. And there had been no guarantee Amelia would accept his proposal, which made the whole background story unnecessary.

'Let's sit,' Massimiliano suggested, gesturing to the table Antonio had recently occupied.

Antonio sat opposite Amelia, and Massimiliano beside her. As with the night before, he eased his arm along the back of her chair, his fingers carelessly brushing her shoulder. Only these chairs were somehow closer, and his whole body seemed to enfold hers with warmth. 'I apologise, *carina*. I was surprised. Your mother—as I knew her—it seems so out of character.'

Amelia's smile was brittle. 'I suppose people change, don't they?'

He shook his head, clearly wanting to say more, but deciding not to. And yet, an instinct to share was burgeoning inside Amelia, surprising her, because she kept so much of this to herself. 'My parents weren't happy,' she said, after a beat. 'I think at first, the romance of their elopement, being young and in love, it all seemed very exciting. But the adjustment was huge. My father was far from wealthy. He'd been in the foster system and had nothing behind him. Apart from his music, he had no real skills, no career.' She lifted her shoulders. 'I'd say the romance wore off pretty quickly, but by then, she was pregnant with me.'

Sympathy softened Antonio's eyes. She didn't look at Massimiliano. She couldn't say why, but she had a feeling that if his face was similarly creased with pity, she might start to cry.

'I wonder why she didn't come home, to Italy,' Antonio said.

She was saved the need of offering an immediate response by the appearance of a waiter, who began to speak in rapid-fire Italian.

More muscle memory. More reflexive pain.

Those words were buried deep, deep inside her, the most obvious connection to her mother. She'd stifled them for so long, and now, they surrounded her. They were being rammed in her face, thrown at her like some kind of assault. She sat up straight, panic knifing her sides.

A part of her that she'd run from for so long, hidden away, and here it was, laid before her, so that as they spoke she saw and heard her mother. Her heart felt scraped raw. She dug her fingernails into her palm, trying not to think about the normal expectation of a wedding day, about the fact her mother should have been there. Both of her parents, in fact. Trying not to think about how alone she was in the world, her only family the couple she'd met last night, for the first time.

Antonio laughed at something the waiter had said and her gaze narrowed thoughtfully.

She was going to be living in Italy for the next two years. Had she really thought she could avoid the language? Wouldn't it be better to face this emotional speed bump head-on and learn to speak it? Perhaps it would even be an exorcism of sorts, like a reclaiming of something she'd associated with her mother for so long that didn't actually belong exclusively to her. In speaking Italian herself, could she erase all those memories of Aria, reading to her, singing to her, in her native tongue?

Massimiliano's fingers roamed her shoulder, and then moved to her hair, curling around the ends, brushing over it. His touch had the effect of driving her troubled thoughts from her mind, leaving only pleasurable trembles in its wake.

He leaned close, his voice delivered right to her ear, so his warm breath breezed across her cheek. 'Would you like me to order for you, *cara*?'

She glanced up at him, and there it was again. Proximity. Closeness. Lava.

Her eyes blinked but neither looked away. His hand shifted from her hair to her cheek, brushing it gently, his eyes following the gesture before falling to her lips, so she sucked in a sharp breath.

He turned away though, and began to speak in Italian, presumably ordering for himself and her, before nodding at Antonio. *'Nonno?'* As the old man began to speak with the waiter, Massimiliano addressed her in hushed tones, his voice deep and husky, his accent like warm butter on her frazzled nerves.

'I'm sorry about your mother.'

She closed her eyes, breathing in, his sympathy having exactly the effect she'd expected it might.

'Thank you.'

'It is not to thank me for. I just wanted you to know that I understand, that you deserved better.'

It was *exactly* the right thing to say. Surprise had her eyes widening. 'As did you,' she murmured.

He dipped his head once, as if to agree with that. 'And yet,' he murmured, lips close to her ear, so that she alone could hear his words, 'I learned so much from my father's actions. About wealth, greed, corruption and, most importantly, human nature. Had he not done what he did, I might have spent my entire life presuming that people were truly, in their hearts, as they appeared.'

'And instead?'

He pulled back a little, so their eyes met. 'I trust no one.'

A shiver ran the length of her spine, but it was snuffed out by the heat he was generating, by essentially wrapping his far larger body around hers.

'I get that,' she said. Inside, she was nodding, but she made a conscious choice not to shift her head, because it might break the spell of being near to each other. Even as, in the back of her mind, she forced herself to remember that this was all for show. It didn't negate the fact it felt incredible.

'Somehow, I don't think you do,' he drawled, eyes hooked to hers in a way she found impossible to look away from.

'Why do you say that?'

'Because you are soft where I am hard.'

She frowned. His English was excellent, but she didn't fully understand. 'What does that mean?'

'That you cannot, I think, help giving people chances. Letting them in.'

'You're wrong.'

His lips lifted in a cynical half-smile. 'Am I?'

'I have literally no friends and no family,' she muttered. 'I am completely alone in the world.'

He leaned closer, so now his lips brushed against her ear. 'Except for me.'

She shivered then, from warmth and longing. 'For two years,' she said. 'And only in name.'

His face hovered where it was, so close her insides twisted with awareness, and then he pulled back a little, so they could once more look into each other's eyes. Her heart turned over, as silently she implored him to say something that might dispute that.

He didn't.

A moment later, the waiter left, and Massimiliano expanded the conversation to include his grandfather. Amelia pretended she didn't mind.

CHAPTER SEVEN

'YOU'RE RIGHT. HE'S GREAT,' Amelia said as Massimiliano's limousine cut a path across Rome. She glanced towards her window, regretting the change in scenery. While this part of the city was undeniably more beautiful and picturesque, she'd loved her time at the trattoria. The food had been, as Massimiliano had promised, exquisite. She wasn't sure she'd ever eaten anything quite so delicious, in fact. From the squid-ink pasta entrée to the courgette flowers that were served deep fried and stuffed with soft goat's cheese on the side, to the aubergine and prosciutto Parmigiano stack she'd enjoyed as a main course. While Massimiliano and Antonio had opted for short black coffees for dessert, served with a bitter almond biscuit, Amelia had chosen a tiramisu, and it had been prepared fresh at the table.

She wasn't sure she'd ever need to eat again, however.

'He liked you, too.'

Her eyes lit up as she turned to face him. 'How can you tell?'

'Because he's my grandfather, and I know him.'

Warmth wrapped around her.

'I'm more like you than you realise,' she murmured, toying with the bottom of her blazer, running a finger over the discreet stitching. 'I keep people at a distance, as a matter of course. It's just so much easier not to rely on anyone,' she pointed out. 'I go out of my way not to like people. Not to want them to like me. But he has a way of breaking down your barriers.'

Massimiliano's eyes, when she glanced up at him, were boring through her, as if weighing the truth of her words.

'Yes,' he admitted, finally, giving very little away. 'He is open and charming. What you see is what you get.'

'He must have taken things with your father very hard.'

Massimiliano didn't react physically, as she might have. He simply nodded slowly. 'It was a betrayal on every level.'

She was silent, wondering if he'd continue, not wanting to spook him away from doing so.

'My grandfather raised my father to follow in his footsteps. To share his values, his beliefs. To be just like him. But where Antonio is scrupulously honest, my father lied as easily as he breathed. He was deceitful for the sake of it.'

She gasped. 'I can't imagine that.'

'That doesn't surprise me. You are too inherently good, I think, to appreciate the existence of pure evil.'

'You think your father was pure evil?'

His eyes narrowed when they met hers, and a muscle throbbed at the base of his jaw. 'The definition of it.'

'Was there more?'

'More than stealing from every single person we knew, pocketing their money and then running away like a coward, to leave my grandfather and me to face the consequences?'

She bit into her lip. 'When you put it like that,' she croaked huskily, 'it does sound pretty bad.'

'Yes,' he agreed with a decisive tilt of his head. 'But you're right. There was more. Things my grandfather doesn't know. Things I saved him from discovering, because I didn't see why both of us should have to live with the truth.'

She pressed a hand to her mouth and then reached over, placing it on his knee. Despite the tenor of their conversation, sparks assaulted her inner wrist. 'Do you want to tell me?'

His eyes hooked to hers, loaded with feeling, so her stomach squirmed. She felt his pain like a visceral, intense shock to her system.

'You do not need to be burdened by it either. Suffice it to say, where my grandfather is the best of men, my father was the very worst.' He put his hand over hers, and her heart lifted, except it was only an act of removal. He placed it on the console between them, leaving her whole body ice cold. 'My primary goal in life is to be nothing like him.'

'Another thing we have in common,' she murmured. 'I have spent so long running from my mother, I sometimes don't even know who I am.'

'Anyone else might urge you to try to forgive her, even just in your own heart. But I understand the unique anger that parental abandonment and betrayal can stir up. I understand why you would run from her, *cara*, and keep running. Honestly, I think it's wise.'

She sighed heavily, turning from him to look out of the window, trying not to let it mean anything that he understood her. And that his understanding somehow meant something to her broken, battered heart, though she knew she shouldn't let it.

***

An hour before their wedding, Massimiliano pressed the buzzer for Amelia's hotel suite. Dressed in an impeccable tuxedo, he looked every bit the billionaire groom. And he was surprisingly impatient to see his bride, given the businesslike nature of their engagement. Tradition, of course, dictated that he couldn't see her. That it was bad luck. But going to her hotel was yet another way to underscore the fact this wasn't a normal wedding. It was business.

Except, it hadn't all been businesslike, he reminded himself, thinking of that kiss in his limousine. A stupid move, on his part, because it had built into an obsession in his mind. A dark, sensual need that had made it impossible to think of anything but taking her to bed and making her his, just as she'd asked him to when he'd proposed. It was part of their deal, but it was now also a driving force for him.

He heard a noise behind the door and, a moment later, it was pulled inwards by Amelia.

It was like being punched in the gut.

She looked…so young and innocent. The words slammed into him like an accusation. Her dress was snow white and so traditionally bridal, with a fitted bodice and a full, tulle skirt that fell to her ankles. What he could see of her skin—her arms and back—was flawless, creamy and soft. Her hair was long and loose, styled in curls around her face, and her make-up was light, showing the natural beauty of her features.

But also, again, he was struck by the fact she was only twenty-three, and she looked it.

No, she looked a little like a lamb to the slaughter.

'May I come in?'

She nodded, stepping back, waiting for him to say something, yet he simply stared at her.

'You don't like the dress,' she said, closing the door.

He shook his head, to quickly dispel that idea.

'It's fine.'

Fine? *Do better,* a voice warned. He saw the hurt on her features, the way she withdrew in on herself, and cursed inwardly. 'Better than fine,' he amended, walking towards her, his body vibrating with an electromagnetic force, a soul-deep need to pull her into his arms and kiss her again. To kiss her all over. To remove that pretty, frothy dress and run his hands over her naked body.

'I thought it was bad luck for grooms to see brides before the wedding.'

'That might be true, for real weddings.'

Her expression shifted again. Two for two, he thought, suppressing a groan. And yet, it was the right thing to do, to keep them focused on the truth of this marriage. It would save any future complications to be as business-like about their interactions as possible.

He reached into his pocket and retrieved another velvet box. 'This is for you.'

She looked from his face to the box, her lips quirking in a curious frown. He popped the top and she gasped. 'Oh! It's perfect. It's exactly the same.'

'Yes,' he agreed. 'If it makes you more comfortable, you can wear this instead.'

She reached down and slipped the Moretti diamond from her finger, holding it out towards him. When she put it in the middle of his palm, he had to fight an urge to close his fingers over hers and pull her against his body.

To hell with the dress, the make-up. He just wanted to feel her against him, body to body, soft to hard.

'Thank you,' she said, powder-blue eyes lifting to his. Innocent and shy. His gut twisted. Light and dark. Winter and summer. They were two sides of the same coin, but those two sides were never supposed to meet. In pushing her into this marriage, was he destroying her innocence? Smudging darkness over her light? 'I'll feel so much better knowing it's just a copycat, and not worth a small fortune,' she murmured as she slipped the newly made ring onto her finger.

He didn't tell her that, while it was a copycat, it was still a canary yellow diamond, of perfect quality, that had cost more than an average house. It seemed like something she'd prefer not to know.

'I have settled the agreed-upon amount into your account,' he said, sticking to his intention for coming here. 'If you log in, you'll be able to clear your debts.'

Her lips parted on a breath of surprise, almost as though she'd forgotten the reason they were marrying. 'Thank you.'

'Don't thank me, Amelia. It was our deal.'

'I know, it's just…' She blinked quickly as moisture filled her eyes, and Massimiliano's gut twisted again, sharp and hard. 'I've been so worried about money for so long. For years. I can't believe…it's such a relief.'

And despite his best intentions, he reached out then, his thumb padding across her jaw, then cupping her cheek, stroking her lightly. 'I'm sorry I didn't propose to you a year ago.'

A tear slid from her eye. 'That makes two of us.'

He wanted to fix this. More than giving her money,

he wished he could click his fingers and bring back her father, change who her mother was, do anything to make her smile, as she deserved on her wedding day.

But this is not a real wedding, a voice reminded him, insisting he stick to the professionalism their plan required. Only his body had other ideas as he moved forward, finally doing what he'd wanted since arriving at her suite, and letting himself feel her.

Or feel a hint of her, through the layers and layers of tulle.

Massimiliano was thirty-five years old and, in his adult life, he had known many women. Too many to remember, and none of any particular importance. After his fiancée, all those years ago, he'd made an art form out of sensual, meaningless connections. So much the better if the women he slept with, and then walked away from, were from noble families. Those same families that had shunned his, because of the sins of his father. Those same families that had turned the Moretti name into mud.

But all of those encounters, all of those women, had turned into black shards in his mind, slicing through him accusingly, as he looked down on this beautiful, innocent woman and ached to make her his. No part of him thought he deserved that, and yet, they had a deal. Even without it, Massimiliano knew he didn't have the willpower to resist. She wanted him to be her first, and, so help him God, he would be. Just as soon as they were married, and alone…

The wedding gown had been beautiful, but it had been a huge relief to remove the frothy fabric and step into a far sleeker, lighter-weight cream slip for their post-wedding lunch. Massimiliano had booked a high-profile, ritzy restaurant in a trendy part of Rome. The place was all industrial chic, from its exposed wiring and air-conditioning ducts to polished concrete floor, woodchip tables and bright lighting. But the crowd was unmistakably not industrial. These were Italy's elite, in their incredible couture, and from the second she realised that, she knew why he'd chosen to come here.

To be seen.

Antonio and Massimiliano Moretti with the Rossi family. Two of Italy's oldest names, joined together now in marriage. *Her marriage.*

If she'd been sceptical about the importance of this, seeing the way people responded, the whispers, the attention, would have convinced her that Massimiliano had known what he was doing. Their engagement had been announced in the papers, with a nice little quote from Massimiliano about having found the love of his life and brought her home to her native Italy. There was also some interesting information about her family, things she'd never known, so she'd felt something creaking open inside her, despite her best efforts.

Pride, in the Rossis. Curiosity about their history. Interest in her Italian heritage, and this beautiful, historic country she'd pretended, all her life, simply didn't exist.

The fact Antonio and the Rossis had once been close friends was very easy to understand. The initial awkwardness had faded by the time the first course arrived, and they began talking in rapid-fire Italian, so Amelia couldn't keep up.

Massimiliano, though, stayed close to her, his arm around her shoulders, his fingers doing that now familiar dance, of brushing over her bare flesh, until goose-bumps lifted on her arms.

'How are you feeling?' he asked, when their dinner plates were cleared.

She glanced up at him to find his face only an inch or so from hers. She swallowed quickly. 'I'm fine.'

'I mean about tonight,' he pushed, gently, so her body exploded with anticipation and heat. Embarrassed, though, she dropped her gaze to his chest.

'I wasn't sure if you still…'

His finger pushed gently beneath her chin, tilting her face back to his. 'Still what?'

'If it was going to happen. Tonight, I mean.'

'Do you doubt my word, *Contessina*?'

Her heart dropped out of her body. She bit into her lip, wishing that didn't sting so much. It wasn't until that moment, she realised how much she wanted this to happen, not because of a deal, but because of something between them. What a fantasist, she thought with impatience. There was no way on earth he'd be looking at her in such a manner if she hadn't wedged this requirement into their negotiations.

'No, Massimiliano.' How good she'd got at saying his name. The syllables rolled off her tongue now, almost as though she'd been born to speak it.

'Good girl,' he said, leaning closer and whispering in her ear. 'Because when we are alone, I am going to strip you naked and make you mine, until you are screaming with pleasure. Is that what you want?'

Heat flooded her body, pooling between her legs. She gasped at the suggestive, intense nature of his statement, of the desire in his voice, the raw sensuality of that promise. She pulled back to look at him. His dark eyes were glittering when they met hers, and her stomach seemed to loop in on itself.

'Is that what you want?' There was that command again, that easy authority.

She nodded, not trusting herself to speak.

Beneath the table, his hand curved over her knee, brushing her through the satin of her dress. She trembled, lifting a hand to his shirt and clinging on for dear life.

'Let's not remain here much longer,' he said, eyes shifting over her face then landing on her lips and lingering there. She pressed her teeth into her lower lip, her body riding a shock wave of need.

She nodded her agreement.

Right on cue, a waiter appeared with a small, perfectly decorated *millefoglie*, with delicate layers of pastry and sweet, vanilla-scented cream.

'Time to cut the cake,' Massimiliano murmured, and she was aware of people in the restaurant removing their phones and taking photographs of them as she reached over, cheeks flushed pink, to slice through the confection. The restaurant erupted in spontaneous applause, and then, perhaps for the sake of those watching, perhaps for the sake of tradition, or maybe just because of the heat that was flaring between them, Massimiliano pulled her against him and kissed her, just as he had in the limousine. Hard and desperate. Mouths mashing together, tongue invading her senses until she couldn't think straight and her whole body felt weak, propped up only by his proximity.

She wanted to moan into him. She wanted to climb into his lap. To drag him from the restaurant then and there and start the night ahead. But he pulled away, eyes staring down at her, chest moving with the force of his breath, as the other patrons continued to clap and cheer. Massimiliano then was himself once more, turning and giving a brief wave, before he focused his attention on their table of five, one arm wrapped carelessly around Amelia's shoulders for the rest of the night.

CHAPTER EIGHT

FROM THE MOMENT she slipped into the back of his limousine, her nerves were stretched on tenterhooks, her insides turning to electric shocks and jelly. She didn't even realise she was fidgeting with her fingers until he reached out and put his hand over hers.

'There is no need to be nervous.'

She turned to face him, blinking, shaking her head. She wasn't nervous. That was a far too one-dimensional way to describe what she was feeling. It was an explosion of noise and feeling, an immersion of excitement, anxiety, adrenaline, disbelief and regret. What if this was a mistake? What if sleeping with him made everything complicated, or was just a total let-down? What if…what if…what if…?

'You don't have to do anything you don't want,' he added.

She shook her head again. 'It's not that.' And it wasn't. The moment he said those words, every cell in her body fought against them, rebelling against the idea of him removing the possibility of this. 'I want to do it. I just want it to be over.'

His lips quirked in an expression of cynicism. 'That is not something I've ever heard.'

She flushed to the roots of her scalp, mortified by the gauche comment. 'You know what I mean. I just don't want to be a virgin any more. I'm ready to do this, and be…me, on the other side.'

'You'll be the same person.'

'Yes, and no.'

He reached over then, brushing his thumb over her cheek, eyes hooked to hers. 'Have you never been tempted, *Contessina*, by a man's touch?'

'I told you,' she said, voice wobbly. 'I just didn't have the time for dating.'

His expression shifted infinitesimally. 'That's not what I asked.'

Her brow furrowed.

'Have you never looked at a man and wanted more? Have you never felt that spark of heat that is your body's way of telling you there's something more here? That it should be explored and enjoyed?'

Her mouth went dry at the sensual question, at the heat he so easily invoked. 'Sex has been the last thing on my mind.' Her words sounded defensive, cold, even, when she was anything but.

'And you are sure you would not rather wait, until you meet someone who can offer you something other than this?'

She frowned. 'I don't want to wait. This is just sex.'

'Yes,' he agreed. 'But is that really what you want?'

'Are you trying to get me to change my mind?'

'I'm letting you know it's okay if you do.'

'I'm fully aware of that, Massimiliano. This is my choice; it's what I want.'

He sat back in his seat, his eyes focused on the back of

the seat in front. 'Okay,' he said, tone of his voice giving little away. 'If you are sure, then so be it.'

She was not in the headspace to take in the details of his luxurious penthouse, so she was glad he didn't give her a full tour. There would be time to familiarise herself with her temporary new home later. Time to absorb the space this man lived in. For now, she was practically trembling from head to toe with anticipation.

'So,' she said, standing in the middle of an enormous living room, with white leather sofas, polished timber floors and a fireplace suspended from the ceiling, hanging right in the centre of the sofas. The afternoon light sliced through the space with a golden intensity, making it look like a film set, rather than a home. 'Where's your bedroom?'

His brows shot up and his smile was slow to unfurl. Except it wasn't really a smile so much as a wolfish grin that made her shiver with something better than anticipation: darkness. Warning. A feeling that she was in way over her head and loved that fact.

'You are impatient.'

'You know why.'

'Yes,' he murmured, walking across the room to the bar and pouring two measures of Scotch—one significantly smaller than the other. 'You want it to be over,' he said with a hint of mockery. He carried the cut-crystal glasses across with him, until they were standing toe to toe, then handed the smaller portion to her. She took it on autopilot, shivering when their hands brushed for even a moment. 'You asked me to be your first lover,' he said, swirling his drink in the glass a little, obsidian gaze holding hers. 'For this to happen, you have to accept that it will be my way. Do you trust me?'

Something flared in the centre of her chest. Adrenaline and excitement. 'I barely know you,' she pointed out, glad she'd muted her first reaction of agreement. Because in some weird way, she did trust him. How could that be, when they'd only just met?

'Is that a no?' he pushed.

She lifted her drink to her lips, breathed in the fragrance then pulled a face. It was so strong and masculine. 'Fine, I trust you. I trust you to do what you said, and not to hurt me.'

His eyes flared. 'Only, I'm not going to do what I said.'

Something stammered in her chest and her hand gripped the glass tighter. 'What? You can't back out. I married you on the basis—'

And then his finger was pressing to her lips, to silence her at first. It worked. She clamped them together, staring up at him, breath jammed in her throat.

'I'm not going to sleep with you tonight.'

Her mouth parted as she processed that. 'But we—'

His finger began to trace the outline of her lips, so goosebumps lifted over her entire body. 'You have no experience with men.'

She was only capable of making a garbled sound of agreement.

'No experience with sex.'

She closed her eyes as his finger stopped tracing and the tip of it pressed against the middle of her mouth, breaching the interior and feeling the moistness of her inner lip. Her heart turned over in her chest and her stomach tightened almost painfully.

'The first thing you need to know is that there's so much more to sex than just sex.'

'That makes no sense,' she groaned as he slid his finger further into her mouth, brushing it along her tongue before withdrawing it, so when she blinked up at him and their eyes met, she felt a surge of something powerful and raw.

'It will.' His smile was arrogant confidence personified.

'The second thing you need to know is that you must use your voice. If you are in pain, if I do something you do not like, or are not comfortable with, you need only say and I will stop. Communication is important, okay?'

She nodded, barely conscious of what she was saying.

'We'll start slow.'

'No,' she whispered, tormented by the strength of feelings that were rioting inside her as, for the first time in her life, waves of sensuality threatened to devour her. 'Not slow.'

'Slow,' he said, leaning forward then and taking her earlobe in his mouth, the combination of his lips and warm breath sending her blood pressure skyrocketing, 'can be very satisfying, believe me.' He pulled back to look at her, then lifted his Scotch and drained it in one motion, before moving away to place his glass on a pale timber coffee table.

Her eyes followed the gesture, her body barely able to support its own weight. Which it didn't need to, because he was back a moment later, eyes appraising her.

His hands moved slowly, to the soft silk of her dress, catching it at her hips and lifting it incrementally, so with each shift her skin seemed to catch fire. By the time he had it lifted to reveal her delicate lace thong and naked midriff, she was almost panting with a need to be completely naked.

She wondered if he realised how torturous it was, for him to be moving so slowly. The fabric rustled over her breasts, her nipples tingled in a way she had never known, and then, finally, he glided the dress over her head and dropped it to the floor.

She lifted the Scotch glass to her lips again, needing a burst of grounding reality, and took a single taste. It hit the back of her throat and then flamed all the way down, but she didn't hate it. If anything, it added yet another dimension to this—standing naked in the middle of a room with a man she'd known for only a week, and had just married.

'Are you ready?' he asked, eyes raking her face then dropping lower to her breasts with unmistakably possessive heat.

She nodded, not even sure what she was agreeing to now, knowing only that she would do whatever he asked of her in that moment, if it meant being able to revel in the spark that was bursting between them.

With that single shift of her head, though, he closed the distance between them, his hand sliding into the lace of her thong, so she almost jumped out of her skin when his touch connected with her sex. His eyes held hers. Was that mockery she saw in their depths? Amusement?

She glanced away, embarrassed.

His other hand gripped her chin, drawing her gaze back to his. 'Do not hide from me. Sex is raw and honest—it has to be. Don't resist that.'

Her breath burned in her lungs with each inhalation.

His finger shifted, and began to move, quickly, finding her most sensitive cluster of nerves and brushing it until she was on the brink of something mind-blowingly intense. Then, before she could surrender to it entirely, his fingers shifted again, this time sliding inside her moist core, breaching a space no man had ever touched, so she cried out at the feeling, the invasion, the welcome presence. He was not gentle, and she was glad. The last thing she wanted was to be treated with kid gloves. Besides, he'd told her he would stop if she asked him to—and no way was she going to do that.

Right when she felt as if her world were imploding all over again, he moved both hands to her exposed bottom and massaged her cheeks, fingers pressing hard into her flesh as his mouth dropped to her breast and sucked a nipple deep inside, so the assault on her senses was more overwhelming than she expected. Warm heat was pooling between her legs, the pressure of pleasure almost overtaking her.

'Massimiliano,' she cried out, his name now so familiar to her, so easy to say. 'Please, God, please,' she groaned, not even sure what she wanted or needed, knowing only that this felt so incredibly good, she wanted it never to end. He nudged his thigh between her legs, his thick, powerful thigh, and, acting on ancient, female instincts, she ground herself against him, needing the relief that only that kind of friction could bring. He moved his mouth to her other breast, and while he sucked it deep and hard, he moved one hand to the nipple he'd just tormented, gripping her breast, plucking at her sensitive mound until she was incandescent with heat and need.

'When I fuck you, you're going to come so hard, *cara.*

It's going to feel so good, for both of us,' he murmured, moving his mouth to her ear, so the words hit her like a tsunami.

'Yes, yes, yes,' she promised, for how could she not? Everything about this man was addictive. No. Not this man. Sex. That was all. She was just learning what most people discovered at a younger age. She was a sexual being, and she'd denied herself this pleasure far too long.

'Tell me what you want,' he instructed, moving his stubbled jaw along her décolletage, then flicking one of her nipples with his tongue, before moving his mouth to hers, finally, and claiming it. He kissed her so hard she couldn't think, much less answer his question. But when he broke away to stare down at her, his eyes glittering with dark determination, she shook her head.

'I don't know,' she said, frustrated by her inability to verbalise the thousand currents of desire that were washing through her.

'Do you like it when I touch you here?' he asked, moving his hand between her legs. She dug her fingernails into his shoulder, nodding frantically.

'I really do.'

'Good girl,' he said, so a shiver of intense pleasure ran down her spine. 'Let me show you why.'

And this time, when he ran his fingers over her until need had built to a fever pitch, he didn't stop. This time, he drove her right to the edge then tipped her over it, his eyes on her face the whole time, while the world, as she knew it, splintered apart for ever.

He spoke in Italian when she fell apart, the ancient words that were locked deep inside her somehow familiar and soothing even as rockets of white-hot desire punctured her entire body, flooding her with intense, blinding feeling. There was no other way to describe it. She was suddenly hyper-aware of everything. Every sight, sound, breath: the soft breeze from the climate control of his apartment, the golden rays of the sun causing beams of light to form on the furniture, his masculine, outdoorsy fragrance, the softness of his suit jacket beneath her fingers, the harshness of his shiny belt against her body. The hyperfocus on the ordinary was somehow extraordinary and shocking, so she was almost drowning under the weight of realisations.

She pulled back from him as if gasping for air, even when her body yearned for more. To be close. To be near. To be fully his.

But it was no longer imperative to do that tonight. His insistence on taking a scenic route to sex was suddenly overwhelmingly perfect.

She stood there, arms by her side, staring across at him, dragging in breath, as the world twisted off its axis and then sort of jammed back on. But not in the same way. Everything was different. Awakening. New life forming. She could *feel it.*

He didn't allow her to separate from him for long. He closed the distance swiftly, eyes boring down on hers. 'Have you had enough for today, Signora Moretti?'

Signora Moretti. Mrs Moretti.

Her gaze fell to the ring he'd given her, and her heart slammed into her ribs for a new reason now. The way he said her name was with such heat and possession that, for the tiniest fraction of time—barely a second—it all felt so *real.* So intoxicatingly, dangerously real.

He moved closer still, so their bodies brushed. 'It is a yes or no question…'

Yes or no. Right or wrong. Need or satiation.

Slowly, she shook her head from side to side, fingers toying with the enormous faux diamond, twisting it around and around. 'No,' she said, eyes huge when they met his. 'Show me more, Signor Moretti.'

His eyes flared at that, the heat in them unmistakable. 'What's the magic word?'

He lifted a finger and traced it from the middle of her brow, lower, over her face, to the tip of her nose.

She shivered. 'Please.'

'You are a quick learner.' His voice was thick with his own need, and when he put both hands on her hips and jerked her against him, she felt the jut of his arousal hard to her belly and stars formed in her eyes. An ancient, feminine need had her shifting her hips, just like before, seeking him, wordlessly inviting.

Instead, he pushed his hand between them and, once more, set about shaking the very foundation of her world, so she no longer recognised anyone or anything, least of all herself.

He wasn't surprised she fell asleep. He looked down at her beautiful body, her long blonde hair loose around her face like an angel's halo, her silky black lashes fanning across her cheeks, and reached forward to grab the sheet and drape it over her body. She smiled softly, murmured something, then rolled onto her side, exposing the still slightly bruised cheek, so something fired inside him. A protective instinct that was both familiar and unwelcome.

He stepped back from the bed, walking quietly from

her bedroom, and down the corridor to his own. Dressing in running gear was a way of putting what had just happened behind himself.

Not that he wanted to.

No, if Massimiliano had it his way, he'd be stripping himself naked and sliding into bed beside her, to hell with what he'd promised. He wasn't sure he'd ever wanted a woman more—and that had caught him completely off guard. Because he wasn't supposed to feel that kind of attraction for his bride. That was not what they were. And he'd been so convinced he could manage this. Marry her and treat her like a business partner, a polite acquaintance to be showed off publicly, from time to time, with no need for any further complications.

Instead, he'd watched her fall apart and known he could get addicted to the thrill of that. Her innocence and responsiveness, the way she clung to him as though he was the only anchor in her world.

There was a thrill that came from what he was doing. The ability to pleasure her to the point of mania, of teaching her everything she would need to know about sex. Of being her first *everything*. In every way.

His gut rolled at that, and he slipped from the heavily secured penthouse quietly, stepping out onto the street. He looked down on the Villa Borghese parklands as he began to run, and then to the dusky sky beyond, the city that was preparing for the night ahead. Ancient roofs, the silhouettes of familiar church domes, the city that he'd loved and hated for so long—loved for what it was, hated for what it had taken from him. For the doors that had closed in his face, after his father's actions.

But that was not why he was running. He had energy

he needed to burn, energy that yearned to be poured into the woman upstairs, fast asleep, beautiful and innocent, and utterly and completely in his hands. The woman he'd married, for the sake of his family's name, who, if he wasn't careful, would become all he could think about.

When a hand trailing over her bare shoulder woke her, Amelia stirred, disoriented and confused. It took several seconds to remember the wedding, what had come afterwards, and where she now was. Her eyes quickly travelled the palatial bedroom, with its stunning furnishings, and beyond, to the view of Rome. In the time since they'd arrived, the sky had grown dark, the stars a blanket of diamonds above them, the city twinkling as though etched in gold. And there, beside her, dressed in a different suit, looking freshly showered, was Massimiliano. Her husband. Her eyes fell to the ring again, her stomach contracting as that reality landed with a thud, right beside memories of how he'd pleasured her.

Shyness twisted inside her belly, making it impossible to say the words she felt: join me. Come to bed.

'We have dinner reservations.'

She tried to hide her disappointment. 'We do?'

He leaned down then, palms flat on either side of her, his face close, so her breath hitched in her throat and, of its own volition, her body twisted beneath the million-thread-count sheets.

'It is important to be seen, remember. Our marriage achieves nothing if it is behind closed doors.'

He was right. This deal was about restoring his family's name, and, for whatever reason, marriage to her had the power to do that. She was obligated to carry out her part of this arrangement. Even if she did long to stay right here, with his hands roaming her body anew.

But whatever temptation he'd felt earlier that day, this version of Massimiliano was all business, focused purely on the question of erasing his father's sins from the memory of Italy's elite.

'Okay,' she said, clearing her throat, sitting up a little, then cheeks flaming as she realised she was completely naked. She grabbed the sheet and hoisted it up to her chin.

His laugh was laced with sardonic amusement. '*Cara*, I've seen you naked. My hands have roamed your body.' He leaned down then, the businessman slipping for a moment, leaving her would-be lover in plain sight. 'Do not hide from me.'

He reached for the sheet, eyes holding hers as he tugged on it, reading her the whole time, perhaps to see if she objected to what he was doing. But she didn't. As his hand withdrew the sheet and the cool air ran over her, she shivered, because it was like an inundation of fresh pleasure. It was everything all at once.

'You are too beautiful to hide from anyone, *Contessina*.'

A lump formed in her throat as his words ran over her, warming her in places she hadn't even known she possessed. She had no vanity. She'd had no time for it. No need, either. She existed purely for the sake of survival, and had done so for a long time. But with his fairy-tale billionaire treatment, and the way he looked at her, it was so easy to believe she was everything he described.

CHAPTER NINE

AT THE TIME, the incredible array of clothes he'd bought her had seemed completely over the top. But as she stood in the stall of the ladies' room and listened to the conversation being indiscreetly held by the sinks, she was glad, at least, that she looked as though she belonged in this world.

The women were speaking in English. One accented, so presumably Italian, two American, and they were talking about her.

'I can't believe they're married.'

'You know who she is, right?'

The Italian made a scoffing sound. 'A Rossi—allegedly. Come on, you saw the article. She hadn't even been to Italy until this week.'

'It doesn't matter,' one of the American voices chimed in. 'She's a Rossi. You know what that means.'

The other American spoke next. 'Do you think she knows what she's getting into?'

A husky laugh, and then the Italian spoke, 'Careful, Sasha. You sound jealous.'

'Puh-lease. As if I'd ever have wanted to marry Massimiliano. It's far more fun to call him up and screw him when I get the itch.'

'No more of that,' the other American tsked. 'He's married now.'

'So?' Sasha's voice showed amusement. 'What does that mean to me?'

A clicking noise sounded, the artificial lens sound of a phone camera. Really? A selfie, while they were dissecting her life? At least Amelia was under no illusions as to what her marriage was, but if she had married for love, this conversation would have been seriously hurtful.

Then again, she would never marry someone like Massimiliano for love. She wasn't sure he was capable of it.

Skilful sex, on the other hand…apparently, he had quite the reputation for that. She ignored the acid swirling through her, the way her throat seemed to constrict at the idea of his being able to pleasure whomever he wanted with such skill and aplomb. But how could she ignore it, when it took what had been so incredibly special, and turned it into something ordinary and tawdry?

'You cannot mean you would sleep with a married man?'

'I find it hard to believe he'll be satisfied with her for long. She looks young and dull.'

Amelia's brow furrowed. Dull? How the heck could they know that? she wondered, cheeks flaming. They knew *nothing* about her. She glanced down at her engagement ring, stomach in knots, but strangely reassured by the sight of it. Whatever they might think, she was wearing the Moretti diamond. Or a good copy of it, anyway.

'You *are* jealous. I thought you were seeing that British director, anyway?'

'Ladies, I can walk and chew gum at the same time. Come on, I'm starving.' Their voices continued towards the door of the bathroom, and then disappeared as they exited.

Amelia pressed her back to the stall, staring at the dark blue wall opposite, sucking in several deep breaths to calm her nervous system, before she pushed out, and came face to face with an older woman, fixing perfect, dark red lipstick in place. Amelia's cheeks flamed even hotter at the idea that her mortification had been witnessed by another.

Amelia resolutely ignored the woman, washing her hands before risking a glance in the mirror. The older woman, with her immaculate blonde hair styled into a French braid, met Amelia's eyes and offered a pouty smile. 'Some women are bitches,' she said. 'Don't take it personally. You got the man everyone wants—they're not the last of it you'll have to deal with.' She walked towards her then, putting a hand on Amelia's. 'I knew your mother,' she said, gaze on Amelia's face. 'You look like her, but something tells me you are not the same, in so many ways. You must take care. This—' she gestured to the restaurant beyond '—is a viper's nest.'

Amelia sucked in an uneven breath as her emotions rioted. She wanted to ask this woman about her mother, but she held back, out of a self-preservation instinct she'd honed as a child.

'Thank you,' was all she said, dipping her head once.

'Be careful,' the woman added as she pulled the door inwards, flashing another crimson smile. 'Your husband is no walk in the park, either.'

She was different when they got home. Different from how she'd been that afternoon, like a field of gasolene, ready to be ignited, trembling for his touch. Now, there was a wariness to her, a different kind of ignition being held at bay. She'd been like it for the last portion of their evening as well, her terse smile replacing the natural interaction they'd shared over their meal.

He'd been surprised to find he enjoyed talking to her. Surprised, and rendered a little off balance by it. He hadn't expected her to be so intelligent. So worldly. There wasn't a subject on which she couldn't speak, which had him wondering more about his bride than he wished. Because other than the next few nights, when he intended to seduce her to the point of oblivion, so her sexual awakening was properly completed, this marriage was meant to be no more intimate than the relationship he had with any of his personal assistants.

Professional, courteous, respectful, with obvious boundaries in place.

He didn't want to find himself falling asleep thinking about the little cries she'd made as she'd come for him. Or the reason such a beautiful, well-read woman was working in a diner in the East End of London. He particularly didn't want to be worrying about the way her mood had shifted, and the fact she'd pleaded exhaustion when they'd walked in the door of his penthouse and made a beeline for her own bedroom.

She woke with a strange twisting in her stomach and a heaviness in her heart. A contradiction of feelings. A need for her husband at the same time instinct was telling her to hide from him until she could make sense of things.

But clarity didn't come with the morning. The best she could do was convince herself to focus on the positives of this arrangement, and remind herself that her husband meant nothing to her, and never would. The cultural significance of marriage was so ingrained, it was easy to think that him being 'her husband' somehow gave her an investment in him, and this, when of course that wasn't the case. She was no more his wife than an actress playing a role. She was being well paid for it, and afterwards, when the job was done and his family name restored, his grandfather at peace, she would be free to get on with her life. Her real life. Without Massimiliano in it.

Her stomach clenched at that, already addicted to the powerful sensual fog he was capable of invoking with a single touch.

One thing she'd come to realise was that she couldn't be completely at his whim while she was here. She needed to investigate university courses, but also the niggling thoughts about the Italian language came back to her. She should start learning the language. There'd have to be an app for that, or some textbooks she could order online. Except, she had money now, she didn't need to think of the cheapest way to achieve her goal. She could enrol in a school, or get a tutor. Something that would fill her days over the next two years.

She took her time showering that morning, and dressed with care, the other women's criticism of her ringing in her ears. *Dull.* Yeah, well. You could buy a girl all the designer clothes in the world, but she supposed a leopard really didn't change its spots. There was a pair of expensive jeans in the wardrobe, which she slipped on, with an oversized T-shirt. Her hair, she pulled into a high ponytail, before applying a little lip gloss. Her bruise had completely faded, which meant there was no need to cake make-up on her face.

When she walked into the kitchen, it was to find a note from her newly minted husband, propped against the coffee machine.

Signora Moretti—
Gone to the office. You looked too peaceful to wake.
Call my assistant for a rundown of the house. See
you for dinner tonight.
MM.

Her pulse exploded. The very idea of him peeking in on her while she slept, just to see if she was awake or not, or perhaps to say goodbye, made her whole body catch fire. But the thought of yet another dinner, being trotted out by her husband to show off his Rossi *contessina* bride, made her stomach drop to her toes.

This was their agreement, though, and she was being very well paid for it. Her gaze shifted to the windows, and, at the view of Rome, her heart kicked up a gear.

Coffee beckoned, and then the day yawned ahead of her—a day that was hers to control, hers to fill, however she wanted. She had never been mistress of her own time, free to do what she wished, when she chose. And suddenly, excitement at the possibilities of that made it impossible to feel anything other than pleasure, no matter what. Because Amelia had spent such a long time being beholden to someone or something, having responsibilities up to her eyeballs, that she almost couldn't believe the freedom she now had. A freedom that was thanks to her husband. No matter what, she'd always be grateful to him for that.

Whatever else she might think about Massimiliano, as she dressed for dinner, she recognised two equally strong, competing feelings. Anticipation, as her body sought those same experiences he'd lavished on her the afternoon prior. And pride, that she would not be seen as dull by the haughty women he'd been with in the past.

To that end, she chose an outfit that was the polar opposite of dull. The slinky minidress was a dark blue in colour and fitted her body like a glove. She teamed it with a pair of ankle boots and a faux-fur jacket, styled her hair in loose, voluminous waves, and followed yet another online tutorial to do her make-up. Her lips she painted a deep cherry red, then stood back to admire the sultry effect, with the hint of a smile. She emerged from her room at the same time he strode into the luxurious penthouse, wearing a dark navy suit and crisp white shirt. He didn't see her at first, so she had the opportunity to let her eyes soak him in, reacting privately to how absolutely gorgeous he was, before his gaze lifted and flicked across the room, landing on her with a palpable thud.

Her lips parted—she couldn't help it. Breath escaped her lungs in a whoosh. She fidgeted with her engagement ring, standing right where she was.

He turned, changed direction, began striding towards her. 'Signora Moretti,' he murmured, eyes scanning her face.

She fought the temptation to bite into her lip, to keep fidgeting. But she was nervous. This was such a different look for her, and she realised then it wasn't just for the benefit of the women they might meet at restaurants. This was about her husband, just as much. About wanting him to approve.

But he simply quirked a brow, as if waiting for her to speak.

She didn't. She couldn't. Her mouth felt completely dry.

'Are you ready to go?'

Her stomach dropped to her toes, her eyes followed, landing on the floor between them. 'Sure,' she managed to croak out, ignoring the wave of disappointment, and not letting it take over. 'I'm starving.'

Then his hands shifted to her hips, holding her through the slinky material of her dress. 'That makes two of us.' Except when she glanced into his eyes, she blushed to the roots of her hair, because it didn't feel as though he was talking about food. She had no experience to explain why she felt that, it was simply an instinct. But pleasure exploded through her and heat began to build in her chest.

'Then we'd better go.'

Neither of them moved. His eyes held hers and then, slowly, his hand lifted, to curve around her cheek. 'Are you better?'

She blinked at him, not understanding.

'Last night. You were exhausted.'

'Oh, right,' she murmured. She'd been ruminating on the women she'd overheard, the facets to the man she'd married. She'd wanted space. She'd also really, really wanted him.

'Yeah.' She nodded unevenly. 'I'm all good.'

'I'm glad to hear it.' Then he dropped his hand to hers and laced their fingers together. 'Let's go.'

It was yet another incredible restaurant filled with Europe's elite. Wealthy, well-heeled people who made no effort to hide their interest in Massimiliano's new bride. She felt the surreptitious and not-so-surreptitious attention of the room on her for the entire meal, despite the fact their booth was on the wall at the back of the restaurant.

Despite the fact that her husband had spent the night

in a skilful, slow seduction that had wound her up almost to breaking point. His every touch, every glance, had sparked something inside her, so when he suggested dessert, she wanted to scream 'no'. All she could fantasise about was going home and dragging him to bed. Not for another lesson, either, but for the whole kit and caboodle. She wanted him. Sex. She needed that more than she could say.

'Have you ever had *maritozzi* Amelia?'

His voice was deep, raw. She shook her head, not sure if she could speak. He signalled to the waiter for some to be brought, then topped up Amelia's champagne.

'You look very beautiful tonight.'

Her heart turned over in her chest. Pleasure was a mushrooming cloud. 'Thank you.'

His lips twisted in a half-smile.

'How was work?'

'Satisfying.'

She arched a brow at that. 'You like what you do.'

'I enjoy doing it well.'

It was a fine distinction, but one she appreciated.

'Were you always this driven?'

'I imagine so. I never needed to be until my father's scam was exposed.'

She winced. 'It must have been mortifying for you.'

'Yes.'

She appreciated his candour, the fact he didn't try to downplay it.

'So, is this working?' she asked, looking around the restaurant. To her surprise, it had thinned out, so only a third or so of the tables were now occupied.

'This?'

'Our marriage. Are you suddenly accepted again?'

His laugh was low and husky, and he didn't answer right away, because the waiter appeared carrying their desserts. Little buns filled with cream, and two dark coffees.

'To stave off exhaustion,' he murmured as the coffees were placed before them.

Heat flushed her cheeks as her mushrooming warmth turned into a solar flare.

She reached instead for her champagne and took a sip, then kept her eyes on him. Beneath the tablecloth-covered table, his knee brushed hers and a jolt ran the length of her spine. But it was nothing compared to the complete overwhelm of feeling that ran through her when his hand curved over her knee.

Her eyes flared, but held his.

'I'm playing the long game,' he murmured. 'Uniting our two families is an important step, but it will take time for the sins of my father to be erased.'

'It's been a long time already, hasn't it?'

He dipped his head in agreement as his hand began to creep higher up her bare leg. She sucked in a breath.

'I have never shown any interest in mending the damage he caused, beyond making financial recompense. For my part, I do not care what these people think. Were it not for my grandfather,' he said, lifting one shoulder as his hand crept higher still, 'I still wouldn't.'

'Massimiliano,' she whispered, with urgency, grateful that his much larger frame was on the outside edge of the booth, so when he angled himself fully towards her, resting his elbow on the table, he created a sort of screen from the restaurant.

'But yes, *cara*. Already I have congratulatory phone calls from the sort of people who would not even speak my name twelve months ago.'

'I don't understand why it had to be me,' she said, finding it almost impossible to concentrate when his finger crept to within an inch of the very top of her thighs and began to draw invisible figures of eight.

'Your family is powerful.'

'But there are many other families…'

'The Rossis are ancient. Your grandparents respected and revered. This matters.'

'I just don't understand,' she said, eyes growing hooded as the way his finger was moving became almost hypnotic. He was casting a spell and she was falling under it.

'Yet you agreed to marry me.'

'You're paying me a lot,' she pointed out.

His eyes roamed her face. 'It's worth it.'

'But—' She bit down on her lip as memories of the women in the bathroom haunted her. 'You're the man everyone wants.'

He laughed at that, but it was a deep-throated, cynical laugh. 'Is that so?'

'I have it on good authority.'

'Whose authority would that be?'

She suddenly regretted that she'd started this conversation.

'Contessina?'

She shook her head a little. 'I met your assistant today. She showed me how everything works in your penthouse. How to get security and a driver, that kind of thing. She's also organising an Italian tutor for me. I decided I should learn how to speak the language, you know, if I'm going to be living here.' She was babbling. An effect of his intimate touch, his proximity, and the fact she felt weirdly embarrassed about what she'd overheard the night before, and wished she hadn't brought it up.

His eyes narrowed. 'I'm aware of that, but I find it hard to believe she would discuss my personal life.'

Amelia closed her eyes. He was like a dog with a bone. A very sexy, desirable dog. Beast. Something. 'She didn't.'

He moved then, using his other hand to take one of the petite cream buns, looking at it for a moment before lifting it towards her lips. She glanced up at him, then back at the confectionery as he pressed it to her mouth. 'Taste it,' he murmured.

Heat sparked in her chest but she did as he said, opening her mouth for a bite. It was so sweet, light, fluffy and delicious. She moaned her appreciation. His eyes held hers approvingly.

'Who have you been talking to?'

'No one,' she said. 'I just…overheard some women.'

His eyes scanned her face thoughtfully and then he leaned closer. 'Last night, during dinner.'

She dropped her gaze, nodding once.

'And what did they say?'

She lifted one shoulder. 'That you could have anyone you wanted, basically.'

'I see.'

He reached for the cream bun once more, hovering it against her lips. This time, she bit without being prompted. But as her mouth closed over it, his finger slipped downwards, between her legs, easily navigating the fabric of her minidress and connecting with the lace of her briefs. She gasped, the sensation of the delicious dessert combined with the sheer sensuality of his touch making her see stars already.

'In bed, perhaps. But not the calibre of bride I needed for this to work. And not in the timeline required.'

He'd said something like that in London. That he needed this to be quick, and he needed someone he could essentially bribe into fitting the role.

'But surely one of those women—' She broke off as his finger easily pushed past her briefs and then pressed inside her, making her cry out. He smothered the noise with a swift, hard kiss.

'Massimiliano, someone will see. Take a photo…'

'No, they won't. No one can see you here, *cara*. No one can see past me. Relax.'

But she wasn't relaxed. Every shift of his finger stirred her to a point of intense awareness and need, so beneath the floor-length tablecloth, her fingers gripped his thigh hard, as if that could help her keep a grip on her sanity.

'There is no one from my past that would have been right for this. No one I could marry, without there being an answering expectation of intimacy. Affection. I am not interested in either of these things.'

Her eyes pinged open as her heart did a strange lurch. 'Present situation excluded?'

'This is part of our deal,' he reminded her, moving his finger faster then, deeper, so her hips writhed against him. 'We are both aware of the temporary nature of what we're doing.'

'Yes,' she whispered, but it wasn't really in response to his statement, so much as the way his touch was sending arrows of flame and fire through her body.

He leaned down, whispering in her ear, 'When we

get home, I'm going to strip you naked and kiss you all over. Starting here.' And then she was tumbling over the edge of the earth, into a deep abyss of light and warmth, the soft sound of her orgasm swallowed by the white-hot heat of his kiss.

He had not done anything quite so reckless in a long time. Probably since his early twenties, when the first heady years of his success had kicked into gear, stress of his father's crimes fading just enough to allow Massimiliano to enjoy the riches he'd earned. The women that fell into his lap because of them.

Then, he'd been careless often. Truly careless. He hadn't cared about his own reputation, much less theirs. But Amelia wasn't just some vain socialite he'd picked up in a bar. She was his wife, ostensibly the woman he loved. She was also a virgin.

Making her climax in the back of a restaurant shouldn't have been part of it. *Cristo.* But he hadn't been able to stop himself. He'd wanted her since the afternoon before. He'd wanted her all last night, during dinner, and beyond, when he'd gone to his own bed. And hell, he'd wanted her throughout the day, too, thinking of her when he should have been focusing on something else. Remembering the way she'd responded to him, the innocent, artless way she'd simply reacted to her first encounter of sex and sexual awakening.

It had been a long time since he'd been with someone inexperienced, since he'd seen sex as she must. Since he'd remembered the surprise of knowing your body to be someone else's to command—and be commanded by.

As his car slipped through the streets of Rome, and

his eyes glanced across the familiar landmarks, it was a sense of unfamiliarity that clawed through him. A feeling that marriage to Amelia, while practical and sensible, also had the potential to get out of hand, if he let it. Which he wouldn't, of course. He was Massimiliano Moretti. He'd built an empire from the crumbling ruins of their family's fortune, and he would never let anyone or anything derail his focus. Particularly not some young British woman he'd been required to marry.

CHAPTER TEN

His promise had been a whisper in her mind from the moment they left the restaurant, her cheeks flushed with remembered pleasure but also embarrassment as she looked around to see if anyone was staring at them. Knowing what Massimiliano had just done. He kept his hand pressed to the base of her spine as they stepped out onto the street.

The restaurant was exclusive, and, as befitted such a venue, there was a gaggle of paparazzi waiting to get pictures of whoever exited. The camera lights flashed and Massimiliano immediately pulled her closer to his side, holding her against him, shielding her, just as he had in the restaurant. Making her feel safe. Not alone. Making her feel dangerously close to belonging.

In the limousine, they were both silent, but for Amelia, every single instant was like the stretching of her nerves, so by the time they rode the elevator to his penthouse, she was a tangle of need. If anything, what he'd done in the restaurant had just stirred her up, so she barely managed to make it to the expansive lounge room, on legs that were not at all steady, before she spun around to face him.

But Massimiliano was regarding her with a quirk of his lips that told her he *knew* what he was doing, and she resented that. She wished she were more sophisticated. That she had at least some experience with men. She must have seemed so gauche compared to the women he usually slept with. Her stomach twisted for a different reason now, as self-doubt clicked into her brain.

Then, though, he was striding towards her, his eyes darkening as he got close. 'I seem to remember making you a promise,' he said. As though he sensed that she was suddenly riddled with uncertainty. He stopped, though, a few strides away from her, lifted his finger and crooked it. Inviting her to approach him. To be the one to initiate this.

With those still-trembling legs, she closed the distance between them, and then his hands found the bottom of the dress and began to lift it. As with the afternoon before, it was a torturously slow process. Where she wanted it removed swiftly and thrown to the ground, he delighted in inching it over her body, his hands touching her as it went, before discarding it. Finally.

'I said I'd kiss you all over, I believe,' he murmured, moving his mouth towards her but stopping short of doing any such thing. She tilted her face, silently inviting him to take her mouth with his own, to claim it. He lifted a finger between them, pressing it to her lips.

'I also said I'd start here,' he reminded her, dropping his other hand between her legs, so she yelped at the very welcome, yet unfamiliar, sensation of his touch.

'Massimiliano,' she groaned, tilting her head back.

'Yes, Signora Moretti?'

Forks of awareness threatened to split her apart.

'Please,' was all she could say, even when she had no idea what she was asking for, exactly.

'I promised you,' he reminded her. 'And I never go back on my word, Amelia.'

For the second time that night, Massimiliano did something unusual. Something he hadn't felt an interest in doing with another woman. Not since he'd been a teenager, experimenting with sex. But with Amelia in bed, naked and begging for him, he ached to give her every single ounce of pleasure he could. To flood her body with sensations that were almost too powerful to bear.

'Do you trust me?' he asked, voice dark with intent.

Her eyes lifted to his, and, despite the tugging of her lips, she nodded. 'Yes.'

Something flexed in his chest. 'And what do you do, if you want me to stop?'

'Tell you.'

'Good girl.'

His hands moved to his belt then, removing it slowly from his trousers. Her eyes followed the gesture, her tongue darting out to moisten her lower lip in a way that made some of his seed spill. *Cristo*, but she was beautiful.

'I want to try something, Amelia.'

Her eyes lifted to his face as he came to straddle her, deliberately pushing his cock against her sex so she groaned and twisted her hips, silently inviting him to take her. He leaned forward, capturing first one wrist, and then the next.

She bit into her lower lip as he moved her hands above her head, pinning them between the timber slats of the bedframe.

She kept them there, her breasts drawn towards him because of how he'd positioned her hands.

'I want you to lie there and feel everything,' he said. 'Without touching me.'

She gasped as he began to weave the belt through the bed slats and around her wrists, fastening it with the buckle. She moved her hands reflexively, to test the restraints. They didn't give.

Excitement had his cock jumping.

'Do you understand?'

She nodded quickly.

'I'm glad to hear it.'

And then, because he was a man of his word, rather than kissing her body, as he was aching to, he moved his mouth slowly from her forehead and then lower, keeping his lips a centimetre from her flesh at all times, so only the hint of his breath touched her.

Goosebumps lifted visibly across her, so by the time he reached her legs, she was whimpering and twisting her hips.

He bit back a smile. His hands caught her thighs and moved them wider, exposing her to him completely, and then he buried his face between her legs, tormenting her and tasting her until she was exploding against his mouth, until her cries filled the room, the sound of them as addictive as they were unbearably tempting. But he was a man of his word, and he'd promised her a full sexual awakening. This was just the beginning…

It was some time later when Amelia found she could breathe reliably enough to speak, much less think. Shimmering stars were now a regular feature of her eyes. She'd lost count of how many times he'd brought her over the edge of sanity, with his mouth, his hands, the kisses he'd dragged over her entire body, before he'd released the belt from her hands and kissed her mouth, murmuring against her, 'Okay?'

Okay? She'd wanted to scream. She was so much better than okay. Okay wasn't a word that belonged anywhere in the ballpark of the magical way he'd just sent her over the edge. But she hadn't yet been capable of speech, so she'd simply nodded, collapsing back against the pillows and staring at the ceiling, feeling a little as if she'd run a marathon.

The mattress shifted and she realised he was leaving. 'Sleep tight, *cara*,' he said, winking at her in a way that made her pulse flood with renewed heat.

'You're going?'

'You're not done?' he prompted, raising a brow in a manner that was both sexy and teasing.

She bit into her lip, not wanting to admit that she wanted to see him. To touch and hold him, to explore him as he had her. Not wanting to admit that she wanted to talk to him, to be held by him. But the last two were firmly outside the boundaries they'd established, and as for the first, she didn't know how to ask for it.

'Goodnight,' she murmured, and then, when he reached the door, 'Thank you.'

'Do not thank me for this, Amelia. I am enjoying myself, perhaps more than you realise.'

The next morning was the same as the one prior. He was gone when she woke, with another note propped against the coffee machine.

See you tonight, MM.

* * *

Her heart turned over in her chest at that, but she focused herself on the day ahead. On how to fill the day. Because this was a two-year marriage, and she couldn't just sit around in his sky palace, waiting for Massimiliano to return home and pick up the threads of her sexual education.

She had to keep busy and have a life of her own.

Once they'd slept together, it would be the end of this. That was their deal, and he never went back on a deal.

So she made herself busy, liaising with his assistant to confirm the Italian tutor she'd asked to be arranged, getting the online enrolment forms for her degree and wrapping her head around what she'd need to apply as a mature-age student. Only then did she go out and explore, dutifully using the airphone in his apartment to call for the bodyguards, who she now knew lived in another apartment in this luxurious building, along with his team of drivers.

She spent hours in the historic city centre, walking, exploring and, despite the fact it was a cool early autumn day, buying gelati from a small stall near the *Colosseo*.

She stared up at the arched, ancient building, a heavy thunderclap of emotion moving through her. Surrounded by the evidence of millennia of civilisation, she felt so incredibly insignificant and alone.

Alone, as she was.

It was ridiculous for her to be standing there, wishing, for reasons she couldn't explain, that her husband were with her. Because he wasn't really her husband. No matter what their marriage certificate said, or the articles in the paper, or the way they were in bed, nothing changed the fact that this was a purely practical marriage.

'Signora Moretti?' Her bodyguard appeared at her side, dark glasses covering his eyes. 'You said you needed to be back at the apartment by four?'

She glanced down at her watch, surprised to realise she'd lost hours in her slow, reflective exploration of the city.

'Goodness, yes. Thank you, Pietro.'

'This way, *Signora.*'

The Italian tutor the agency had sent was a young man, perhaps in his mid-twenties, who spoke Italian as his native language, as well as flawless English, French, German and Russian. His name was Christiano, and he was, Amelia came to realise, a perfect choice for someone like her. While she had once held a basic grasp of Italian, she'd actively worked to blot it out, so, to all intents and purposes, she was a complete beginner.

And yet, her palate had been formed around the Italian language, so the slide from vowels to consonants to more vowels was not hard, and her accent, according to Christiano, was excellent.

They covered only the basics, but Christiano suggested a daily lesson, for the first month or so, and Amelia readily agreed. Anything to fill her time, give her a sense of purpose, and have her life be less lonely.

He smiled brightly when he left, and Amelia walked around the apartment practising the verbs he'd taught her that day.

As she was getting ready for dinner, her phone began to ring—her grandmother's name appeared on the screen. 'I'm sorry for interrupting your honeymoon, my dear,' she said, so something twisted inside Amelia. It hadn't even occurred to her that they might have had a honeymoon. It would have been normal, if their wedding were real.

'Can we have dinner next week?'

'Would lunch suit?' Amelia asked, blushing to the roots of her hair when she made the suggestion. Because dinners had become synonymous with Massimiliano, with his slow, determined seduction of her. Though it had been only two nights, she wasn't ready to give away that time together, yet.

'Of course, *cara*. Text me a time and place and we'll be there. *Ciao*.'

'Ciao,' Amelia mirrored, before disconnecting the call, and staring at the clock for perhaps the tenth time that hour. She groaned, because it was all so pathetic and nineteen fifties of her. Somehow, in the space of less than a fortnight, she'd become a woman who obsessively waited for her husband to get home from the office. And he wasn't even her real husband.

He took her to yet another exclusive restaurant with exquisite views and food. Every time Massimiliano looked at her, she felt her pulse explode, and in the back of her mind she wondered if this would be the night. If this would be the night he drew her into his arms and made love to her, so she knew the pleasure of his complete possession, finally.

She didn't want to dull her senses, so she'd had only one glass of champagne at dinner, yet a new sort of courage fired through her when they walked into his penthouse that evening.

'I want to see you,' she said, dropping any preamble.

He turned to face her slowly, eyes glinting like black opals.

'I beg your pardon?'

She hesitated for the briefest second. 'I want to see you naked. It seems only fair.'

'Next you'll be asking to tie me up.'

'Are you saying I couldn't? Isn't that a double standard?'

A smile quirked his lips. 'Yes.'

'Good thing I'm only talking about undressing you, then.'

His eyes bored into hers for a long beat and then he nodded, slowly. 'So, what are you going to do about it?'

Her heart rate kicked up a gear as she strode across to him, her fingers slightly unsteady as she pressed against the lapel of his jacket and eased it down his warm, masculine body. She felt his gaze on her the whole time. Instead of unnerving her, it gave her strength and courage.

Her fingers found his button next, her gaze shifting to his quickly before returning to his chest, with a harsh intake of breath.

'I've never done this before,' she said, needlessly, as she unfastened one button, then another.

'Undone a shirt?'

A smile twisted her lips.

'Undressed a man. Or seen one naked, for that matter.'

She'd seen him without his shirt, in London, but this wasn't the same, and they both knew it.

He made a sound that came from low down in his throat. Sensual and warm, it breathed against her, so she fumbled a little on the last button. But with concentration, she was able to do it. Her hands pushed at the shirt, sliding it down his body, revealing his toned, tanned arms to her hungry gaze. She brushed her palms over his skin, before moving to stand behind him, touching his back, admiring the warmth of him, making her wonder if he spent much time in the sun without a shirt. Without anything. Impatiently, she moved back to the front, finding the belt, wondering if it was the same belt he'd used the night before, warmth spreading through her at the very thought.

She pulled it loose and glanced up at him. 'Want to hold onto this for later?' she asked, in the back of her mind shocked by how forward she was being.

'An excellent idea.' He dropped the belt to the ground beside them though. Amelia moved her attention to his trousers, her nipples tingling almost painfully as she unfastened the button and then the zip, and began to ease them down. He stepped as she pushed the trousers lower, freeing himself from them completely, so he was standing in a pair of black boxer briefs, and her pulse went completely erratic at the final hurdle.

'I'm nervous,' she said, honestly, glancing up at him.

'It's your first time.'

Her heart tripped.

'Nerves are normal.'

She nodded, because he was right.

'You never have to do anything you don't want.'

'I know that.' And she really did. At no point had she ever felt strong-armed into the physical side of their relationship. Where he'd been willing to pull whatever levers he could to arrange this marriage, his incentives and requirements had all been financial. It was Amelia who had demanded this physical intimacy. If anything, she was the one who'd pressured him.

She glanced up at him, a small doubt flickering in her belly. 'The same goes for you, you know.'

He arched a brow, silently encouraging her to continue.

'You don't have to do this, if you don't want to. I know I said it was a condition, but you can't really obligate someone to sleep with you.' Her lips pulled to the side as she heard herself let him off the hook. 'I don't know what I was thinking.'

He nodded slowly, his expression unreadable. '*Cara*, do you still want me to be your first?'

Her eyes flared to his as she nodded, not trusting herself to speak.

His hand moved though, wrapping around her wrist and drawing her lower, to the jut of his cock. He wrapped her fingers around it, through the fabric of his briefs, so she gasped, because it was so big and so hard. 'This is for you,' he said, simply. 'Believe me, you are not forcing me into anything I don't want.'

Her heart pounded against her ribs.

'I want you,' she said simply, so his eyes seemed to shift, showing a hint of hesitation, before he was reaching down and lifting her up, carrying her against his chest, towards her bedroom.

He knew he should go slowly. The whole point of this was awakening her, night by night, bit by bit. But Lord knew, he'd already had the patience of a damned saint. He'd taken two slow nights to stir her body, to show her that sex was so much more than the act itself. But now, on the third night, with his wife's pleas ringing in his ear, he could wait no longer.

He removed her clothes so much faster than she had

his, regrettably tearing her dress in the process, as he brought his body over her and began to kiss her skin, aching to tie her wrists again. But for this, he needed to know she could touch him, touch herself, touch whatever the hell she wanted.

And she did. Her hands roamed his body, her nails digging into him, as he brought her so close to climax she was crying out. Only then did he sheathe himself and hitch his cock at her sex, aware that his size was a possible problem for them, being her first time.

'Remember,' he said, holding her legs wide, eyes lancing hers. 'You tell me what you feel. What you need, what you don't.'

She nodded, frantically. 'Please, just please, don't make me wait any longer.'

He'd meant to go slowly, to nudge into her, but her words were so desperate he felt his control slipping, so he buried half of himself in her before getting a grip of himself once more and pausing to check on her.

She nodded, cried his name, and then it was Amelia who moved her hips, drawing him deeper, until an unmistakable, invisible barrier met him, and he felt her stiffen, so he swept down and wrapped her in his arms, murmuring words of reassurance in Italian into her ear, gently easing himself out of her and then slowly back in, so she could get used to the feeling. It didn't take long before she was arching her back and crying his name again, and he no longer felt a need to go slowly. In fact, with every desperate roll of her head and arch of her back, she was begging him to take her harder and faster, so in the end, he did just that, driving into her until they were both wild and thrashing on the bed, the pleasure engulfing them almost too much to bear.

And then, when she came, and her muscles squeezed him so tight he thought he might pass out, he was powerless to resist his own powerful orgasm. Or to ignore the unwelcome thought that formed in that moment: that he could happily do this every single night for the rest of his life.

CHAPTER ELEVEN

'I FEEL LIKE I've been living in a dream, all this time,' she said, eyes closed. But not because she was tired, so much as processing, everything. Every single feeling that was humming inside her, begging for release.

'How so, *cara*?' he asked as those big, strong arms lifted her to his chest, carrying her so easily to the palatial bathroom. He set her down inside the open-plan shower, then flicked a tap, holding his hand under the water until it was warm enough before easing her backwards, into the spray.

She closed her eyes again as the water beaded against muscles and skin that were newly awakened, a body that had been transformed by his touch.

'A dream?' he prompted, naked, running his index finger down her nose, to her lips. She sighed softly.

'Up until this moment, I've been a shadow,' she tried again, to articulate her meaning. 'Only halfway to the woman I was meant to be. I know it probably sounds silly, it's just… I never knew that someone could make me feel like that.' Her eyes probed his, swimming in their depths. 'Is it always this way?'

A muscle jerked low in his jaw as he continued to

stare into her eyes. 'Sex has a powerful way of connecting people,' he said.

The answer was honest, but unsatisfying. Because deep down, she wanted him to admit that this had been different and unique. Special. It should have been a warning sign that she was in over her head. Yet as he reached for a loofah and began to reverently sponge her body, the sound of her own sensations drowned everything else out. Common sense was as dead as desire was alive, raging inside her, and she couldn't bring herself to care.

In the light of day, Massimiliano faced a difficult decision.

To stick to their original deal, or to ask Amelia if she would alter it.

After all, their agreement had been for one night, he'd eked out three. Their agreement had been to have sex, so she could rid herself of the virginity she no longer wanted: he'd obliged.

But as he dressed for the office, every single cell in his body was urging him to stop putting clothes on and slide into her bed. To draw her to him and kiss her awake, to gently coax her body back to the pleasure he knew he could deliver. To lie beside her, kiss her, taste her. Hear her scream his name once more…

It was the strength of his need that eventually drove him out of the door of his penthouse. The force of his need that made him realise he was getting into dangerous waters. Because she was his wife for the next two years, but it was a meaningless marriage of convenience. Little more than a business arrangement.

Blurring the lines with sex hadn't been his choice.

Not that he regretted it. But he would, if he weakened and continued to seek her out. He would if he let this get out of hand. For both of their sakes, he had to get things back on track now, reminding them of the nature of their relationship.

He thought of her all day though. He even contemplated calling her, to see how she was. How asinine! As though they were old friends, or more.

Instead, he worked late, until eight o'clock, planning to be home for just long enough to greet her before leaving for dinner. It seemed like a sensible way to avoid temptation—by avoiding her.

For one week, he seemed to barely notice she was there, apart from their dinners, which he clearly thought to be an obligatory part of gaining acceptance back into Italy's high society. Dinners where he sat opposite Amelia and made cold small talk, asked polite questions about her day. Dinners where she sought a hint of the man she'd started to know, the passion just beneath the surface. But even when their hands brushed accidentally, he was nothing if not polite, barely glancing at her, so she had the sinking suspicion that his whole seduction routine had been just that: a routine. An act. Part of the deal.

I never go back on my word.

The days were lonely, and long. No matter how much she filled them with—and she fitted a lot in—they seemed to be a form of stasis, while she was waiting for the man she'd married to return. She no longer thought of him as her 'husband'. It was a small point of difference, but 'the man she'd married' more accurately encapsulated the emotional estrangement of their situation.

She lunched with her grandparents twice in that week, and put a brave face on, pretending, as he required of her, that she was happily in love with Massimiliano. She sensed the tension in her grandparents, and, thanks to Massimiliano, understood the cause of it. Their finances were disastrous, but he was going to help them.

She poured herself into the Italian lessons she was undertaking with Christiano, combining them with podcasts and audiobooks in Italian, as well as a language app daily. Not to mention, going out into Rome and listening to the language being spoken, letting it breathe into her.

Two weeks after sleeping together, she got a message from Massimiliano's assistant that someone from a glossy Italian fashion magazine was coming to conduct an interview the following day, offering to book a stylist to do Amelia's hair and make-up first. She demurred. She had every intention of playing the part of his wife to perfection, but when it came to how she looked, she preferred to have complete control.

She moved her Italian lesson forward by an hour on the day of the interview, to allow enough time to prepare, but was only halfway through the tutorial session when she heard the front door open and glanced up to see Massimiliano stride into the room. Her heart lurched into her throat, because she wasn't prepared, and her cheeks flushed in automatic response.

Usually, she knew when he was coming home, and had a chance to prepare herself. To brace for impact, so to speak. Her barriers were down, because things with Christiano were so easy and natural, and she was utterly relaxed with him. So seeing Massimiliano unexpectedly hit harder than she would have liked. Harder than she could even admit to herself.

'*Cara,*' he murmured, eyes boring into hers as he squared his jaw.

Her heart was racing. 'What are you doing here?'

His gaze narrowed imperceptibly. 'In my home, where I live?'

She sucked in a breath, belatedly remembering their pretend marriage and forcing a smile. 'I just meant, so early in the day,' she covered, unevenly, moving to stand, hesitating for the briefest moment before walking towards him and lifting up to kiss his cheek. But he angled his head and claimed her mouth instead, his arm coming around her waist to hold her to his body.

All her senses rejoiced. Every single last one of them, at this unexpected, glorious proximity. At his possessive hold. His harsh, desperate, hungry kiss. A kiss that spoke of the need that had been tormenting her for what felt like an eternity.

'Massimiliano,' she whispered, his name a plea and pledge.

'And who is this?' he asked, his voice barely disguising a darkness she hadn't heard before from Massimiliano. But she recognised it anyway. She recognised it from her parents' arguments, over her mother's 'friends'. She heard the unmistakable tone of jealousy and glanced up at Massimiliano, then over to Christiano, who'd begun packing up their books.

'Oh. Christiano—' She blinked quickly. 'I'm sorry, I don't know your surname.'

'DeLuca,' he supplied, with an easy, lopsided grin.

'Christiano is my Italian tutor.'

Massimiliano glanced down at her sharply. 'I didn't know you had started that.'

True, she hadn't mentioned it. It was a difficult thing for Amelia to navigate, given her complex relationship with the language. But in the back of her mind, she knew it was also because she'd had a childish desire to surprise him with her fluency, when she'd grown stronger.

'Amelia is a gifted learner,' Christiano said, then flicked his gaze—and smile—to Amelia. 'If it weren't for your medical aspirations, you'd be a great linguist.'

Massimiliano's eyes seemed to pierce her completely.

'Thank you, but you make it easy,' she said as Massimiliano's hand dropped from her side, his hand stretching at his thigh.

'We have an interview,' Massimiliano said, dismissively, stalking towards the front door.

Her jaw dropped at his rudeness. He couldn't make it any clearer that he wanted Christiano gone.

Amelia shook her head in silent apology but Christiano waved his hand to silence her, winking as he passed. 'Usual time tomorrow?' he asked, not realising that the question was clearly poking the Italian billionaire bear.

'Um, yep. Yeah, thanks.'

Massimiliano only nodded curtly as Christiano left the penthouse. He stood there, then, like a piece of stone, staring straight ahead, leaving Amelia with a thousand and one questions.

She had never really understood that expression about the air being thick enough to cut with a knife, until then. It seemed to take on a volume that was completely different from usual. She couldn't breathe without feeling as though foam were occupying her lungs.

'Massimiliano?' she asked, stomach lurching when he turned to face her. His face was unmistakably angry. So angry she couldn't fathom it.

'I should have been clear, Amelia. While I respect your autonomy, and desire to further your sexual education, doing so in our shared home is both crass and disrespectful. You have money now; you can arrange a hotel room for this.'

Every single part of her exploded with rage. Even though she'd known he was jealous, she hadn't expected this sort of accusation.

'How dare you?' she screamed, at the top of her lungs, angry tears misting her eyes. The stress and rejection of the past two weeks were loaded into those three single words. She heard her voice as if from a long way away, a tormented, furious sound, chilling her to the bone. Because in that moment, she felt more like her mother than ever before. Reacting with emotion, rather than thought. Arguing, rather than walking away, or pacifying.

'He is my Italian teacher,' she said, through the tears, still so angry, but also overcome by pent-up emotion. By all the feelings of rejection she'd experienced since those blissful nights they'd shared. It was as if a volcano had suddenly roared to life and were ejecting lava across the entire room. 'We've been working together for weeks. Your assistant booked him for me. He is someone I consider to be a friend, but, my God, it is not romantic, it is not sexual. How can you even say that?'

He stood his ground, staring down at her, not reacting at all. Not to her tears, nor to her words. 'Because I know you,' he said, after a beat. 'I have seen what a sensually demanding woman you are. Two weeks since we slept together, it's natural that you would be wanting to explore that side of yourself more. Only please, as I say, consider an alternative location.'

She stared up at him in absolute shock. 'I can't—I can't believe you—that's—'

'I will not bring women here, Amelia, rest assured. I'm only making sure we play by the same rules.'

She felt her whole world spinning completely out of control. She shook her head quickly, unable to think of anything to say, then spun on her heel and stalked away from him.

Fuck.

Not only had that escalated quickly, it had exploded way out of his control. He'd walked in and seen his beautiful wife with her head bent so close to another man's, laughing at something he'd said. The other man, objectively handsome, much closer in age to her. Something inside Massimiliano had snapped. A part of him he hadn't even known existed. Not once had he felt possessive of a woman. Even his real fiancée, all those years ago. Not once had he felt jealous.

It had caught him completely off guard, and rather than admit that to her, rather than be placated by her explanation, he'd gone out of his way to say whatever he could to cover his tracks. To make it seem as though he were approaching their situation from an etiquette consideration, rather than one of the basest emotions people were capable of.

He flicked his assistant a text, asking her to reschedule the interview and photoshoot, then poured himself a Scotch. He held it, staring out at the city, replaying the godawful scene in his head, knowing he had to fix the mess he'd just made, until he became conscious of a faint noise behind him.

He turned on autopilot to see Amelia walking through the room, dragging a small suitcase with her. The world seemed to tip sideways. Her face was pinched, a mottled pink.

He hadn't seen his father leave. The coward had slipped out of their home in the middle of the night, leaving no note, nothing to indicate where he was going. But the same feeling of abandonment was spearing him in the side now. How absurd, given they'd met so recently. It gave him a thousand and one reasons to let her go.

Wasn't this what he expected the people in his life to do? To leave? Wasn't that a huge reason he'd spent the last sixteen years keeping people at arm's length, rather than getting attached? Because abandonment hurt like hell. Being left stung. So he should let her go, get it over with. Like ripping off a plaster. At least then he'd know he was through it—that she was just like everyone else in his life.

But even as he hardened in that resolve, he was rejecting it. Letting Amelia go like this was untenable. He wouldn't do it.

He kept his voice measured, even when his insides were rioting, dragging him from one side to the other, in a constant state of flux over what he wanted, and what made sense. 'Where are you going?'

'I'm sorry about the photoshoot, but I can't stay here,' she said, without looking at him.

'I've rescheduled it.'

She nodded once, kept walking.

His gut fell out of his body. He couldn't let her leave.

It was as simple as that. Not without at least asking her to stay, first.

'Amelia.' Desperation meant he spoke her name more curtly than he'd intended, but she stopped walking and finally glanced somewhere in the vicinity of his direction. 'Where are you going?'

'You're the one who reminded me I have money now. I can book a hotel.' His insides twisted. All his life, he'd protected himself from this, but in this moment, when he needed to wrap those barriers around himself harder, tighter, he mentally rejected them outright. 'I don't need to stay here and be spoken to like that.'

'Amelia—'

'No.' Now she looked at him, and the loathing and pain in her eyes sliced him in half. 'You bought me. I'm your wife. But you have no right to yell at me, to speak to me as though I'm some cheap, sex-obsessed woman who can't wait to move on to her next conquest. You have no right to treat my friend as you did this afternoon. If you think I'm going to stick around and wait for you to say something else like that, then think again. I will not be treated—'

'You're right,' he said, knowing immediately that he had gone so far over the line of acceptability, she was doing the only thing she could.

He put his drink down quickly and crossed to her, hating the way she seemed to pull back from him even before he reached her.

'My behaviour was disgusting. I had no right to say those things, to act that way. I'm truly sorry.'

She shook her head, lips compressed.

If he was going to fix this, he had to be completely honest. 'I was jealous.'

Her eyes lifted to his but slipped away again, just as quickly. 'I'm not completely stupid. I guessed as much. But sleeping together once doesn't give you a right to dictate who I can spend time with. We're intending to be married for two years; are you saying I can't have friends over?'

Male friends, when he wasn't home? That was most definitely his preference, but he recognised the absolute unfairness of that. Particularly when he'd predicated the whole marriage agreement on their freedom to continue discreetly pursuing relationships outside their situation.

The idea of that was anathema to him now.

Why would he want another woman in his bed, when he could have Amelia?

Except that was far from certain, right now.

'I'm sorry,' he repeated, hands on hips. 'I don't think I've ever been jealous before. Evidently, I don't know how to handle it.'

She wrapped her arms around her chest, looking so frail that a part of him broke apart.

'I don't think I can do this,' he said as realisation unfurled in his gut. He felt the danger of what he was about to suggest, the perilous situation he was preparing to step into. But he genuinely couldn't see an alternative, besides letting her leave, and *that* he had already discounted.

'Do what?' she whispered, so softly he barely heard.

'I don't want to think of you seeing other men.'

She shook her head, consternation in her expression. 'I never had any intention of cheating on you.'

His gaze narrowed.

'I know this is just a fake marriage, but I'm not someone who can pretend those vows don't matter.'

He ignored the flare of triumph and assurance her words brought, because it was a house of cards. Her declaration should have been reassuring, yet he felt the earth wobble beneath him. Because it wasn't based on her wanting to be married to him, wanting to be faithful to him. It was the cage he'd built for her, without intending to.

'We have two options,' he said, slowly, realising that there was another door he hadn't considered. One he hated the thought of going through, even while he knew he had to hold it open for her.

'Beyond me going to a hotel for the night?'

'That doesn't solve anything.'

'So what does?'

He stared down at her face, knowing the right thing was to let her go. To get her out of this mess of a situation he'd created.

'If you'd like, you can leave me permanently. We'll divorce,' he said, rejecting that but knowing he had to offer it.

She closed her eyes. 'I can't, and you know why. My grandparents…'

The pain washing over him was like acid burn. He swallowed quickly. It wasn't about him, them, their marriage. Nor should it have been. Still, the ferocity of that rejection cut him. 'I will honour the terms of our agreement. Contrary to my behaviour in the last half-hour, I'm not a cruel man. I have no interest in seeing an elderly couple financially destroyed.'

She sobbed softly.

'You said there were two choices.'

'Stay.'

She looked up at him, biting into that sweet lower lip of hers, full and pink.

'So you can keep ignoring me?' she whispered. 'So you can trot me out each night, your token society bride, for the world to see, then go back to pretending I don't exist?'

'No,' he said quietly. 'And if you think I've been ignoring you, you're wrong. You have been in here,' he said, pointing to the side of his head. 'Like a fever dream. You have breathed yourself into my soul, and I hate it every bit as much as I know I cannot fight it. I am obsessed with you. You are here.' He tapped his head again, more urgently now. 'Every moment of every day.'

She gasped.

'What does that mean?'

'We need a new agreement,' he said, carefully. Years of living with his experience of abandonment had shaped him in ways it was impossible to remove. He was not a man who could emotionally put himself on the line. But for Amelia, he would come as close as possible, if it meant her remaining under his roof.

'Which would be?'

'I want you in my bed,' he admitted, the words dragged out of him, a dangerous territory for Massimiliano. 'Every night that you'll give me.'

She stared up at him, face a mask that gave nothing away. Or perhaps it was that he was so consumed by his own feelings, he couldn't perceive hers.

'And?'

'It's a negotiation,' he said, carefully. 'What do you want in exchange?'

'For as long as we're sleeping together, you won't see other women.'

Disgust flooded him at even the idea of that.

'I'll do you one better,' he said. 'For as long as we're married, I will be faithful to you, as you've said you will be to me.'

'Whether we're sleeping together or not?'

In the back of his mind, he admired the boundaries she was establishing. The way she was reminding them both that two years was a long time, and there was no reason to think this sexual infatuation would last.

It was a reminder that he should not be implementing emotional expectations into their agreement.

'I don't want to hurt you,' he said, stuffing his hands into his pockets to stop from touching her. 'My concern with this is your age and inexperience.'

'I thought we'd dispensed with my lack of experience.'

He shook his head once. 'I mean emotional inexperience.'

She blinked up at him.

'The sex between us is unlike anything I've ever known.'

'I thought it was "normal".'

'Did I say that?'

She frowned. 'I think you implied it.'

He remembered then, how she'd asked him in the shower if it was always like this, and he'd brushed the question off with some line about connection. 'Your question caught me off guard.'

She rolled her eyes and, despite the tenuous situation they were in, a flicker of amusement sparked in his chest. When was the last time someone had rolled their eyes at him?

'But sex is still just sex, *Contessina*. Even with a beautiful woman who has taken over your every waking, and sleeping, thought.'

She nodded slowly. 'You're worried I'm going to fall in love with you.'

He dipped his head once.

'Frankly, I think you should be more worried about that for yourself,' she pointed out archly. 'You're the one who went all diabolical caveman because I was innocently studying with some other guy.'

He smiled at her description, but sobered quickly, because he was still fast-walking over quicksand.

'I'm not going to fall in love with you,' she said.

'How do you know?'

'Because I'm not stupid. I have plans beyond this marriage, and they don't include you.'

'I'm glad, Amelia. Clearly there are things about me that I didn't realise, things about myself I didn't know, but this is not one of them. I decided a long time ago that love and marriage were not for me, and I will never change my mind on that score—nor allow it to be changed.'

She simply stood there, so impatience chewed its way through his gut, making him doubt her, him, the wisdom of this. In the back of his mind, though, he knew that this infatuation would fade eventually. No passion remained at this intensity for long.

Once they were through this phase, they'd drift apart of their own volition. It was the way of things. He was sure of it. As sure as he was of the fact he couldn't fight this any longer. He needed her in a way that was killing him to ignore.

'Amelia, I'm sorry,' he said, again. 'Please, stay.'

'You gave me two options,' she reminded him, but she

took a step closer, pressing a finger to his abdomen. 'I'm still considering them.'

His eyes flared as her finger began to snake downwards, towards his belt.

'Is there anything I can do to help you make up your mind?'

'Oh, I'm absolutely sure there is, Signor Moretti.'

He didn't need to be asked twice.

CHAPTER TWELVE

THE HOT TUB on the wraparound balcony of Massimiliano's penthouse was utterly sublime. Or maybe that was the hour they'd spent before, making love as though they had been separated for years, not weeks. As though they'd been born for the sole purpose of coming together.

There'd been a shift.

She felt a thousand miles away from the virgin she'd been when she'd agreed to this marriage.

And for the first time since marrying, they'd agreed not to go out. Amelia was glad. While being wined and dined around Rome didn't sound onerous, it was nice not to need to get dressed up, aware that all eyes in a venue were locked on her, the women sometimes staring daggers.

She sighed contentedly as her eyes chased the skyline of Rome, marvelling at the famous landmarks she could pick out from where they were, the beauty of this ancient city.

'You know, I always swore I'd never come to Italy,' she said, shifting her gaze to his face as her heart gave a little jolt. He was just too handsome. Especially now, with his hair wet and slicked back from his brow, the top half of his hair-roughened chest exposed to her. His dark eyes locked to hers, probing.

The lights on the deck glowed gold, casting them in a warm ambience.

'Because of your mother?' he pushed, when she didn't elaborate.

She reached for her prosecco and took a sip. 'Yeah. I pretty much rejected everything to do with her when she left.'

'How old were you?'

'Just a girl. And she was my whole world,' Amelia murmured. 'I worshipped her. Then one day, she was just gone.' He made a gruff sound in his throat, a noise of sympathy. Her eyes shifted back to the view, but in her mind, she was drifting into the past. 'They fought a lot, my parents. I think Mum got caught up in the romance of meeting |Dad, rebelling against her parents. Eloping. And then she was pregnant with me. Maybe if she hadn't conceived, they'd have split sooner.' She swallowed quickly.

'What did they fight about?'

'My mother had a lot of male friends,' she said, not trying to make it sound pointed. 'Looking back, I'm pretty sure she had affairs, though my dad never said as much to me. But as an adult, remembering the tenor of their arguments…'

'Which makes how I reacted today even worse.'

'It made it familiar,' she said. 'My dad was pretty chill, except when they fought about her "friends".' A plane flew overhead, a distant, rumbling jet engine noise that drew her gaze upwards. 'I suppose it's why I knew that when I agreed to marry you, I would honour the sanctity of that institution, even when we weren't, you know. A couple.'

She glanced at him, to find his eyes simply resting on her face, his expression inscrutable.

'Anyway. Neither of them was happy. My mother's infidelity wasn't the only problem. I mean, we had no money. That was stressful. And then, one day, she just disappeared.'

Beneath the water, his foot reached out and rubbed her calf, so she flicked a half-smile in his direction. 'I stopped speaking Italian. I removed any photos of her from the house. Any gifts she'd given me. I was so mad, Massimiliano—I swore I'd lose any part of me that was Italian.'

'Understandably.' His toe moved up to brush her thigh, sparking flames in the pit of her stomach. 'So what changed your mind?'

'You can be pretty persuasive.'

'Me, or the money I was offering?' he teased.

She ignored the way her stomach lurched, the immediate instinct she had to reject that. 'Both,' she said in the same spirit.

His expression shifted. 'And learning Italian?'

Memories of that afternoon came back to her. His jealousy. She ran her fingertips over the water's surface, feeling the bubbles pop beneath them. 'I'm not doing it for my mum,' she said. 'If anything, it's for my dad. He always wanted me to stick with it. To keep talking Italian. Losing him, it's sort of made me think about the anger I've held, and I guess, made me want to be everything he thought I could be. Plus, I'm here for two years, so it does make sense.'

He dipped his head in acknowledgement of that. 'Why didn't you say anything?'

'It never came up.'

He nodded slowly. 'And your medical studies?'

For a long time, becoming a doctor was all she'd thought about. Strange, now, that it felt ephemeral. 'Ever since I was a girl, I've wanted to be a doctor.'

The surprise on his face was obvious. 'This is what you're planning to study?'

She nodded. 'About a year before Mum left, my best friend died. She had leukaemia. It was the first time I faced death, and I was too young, really, to fully understand it. I just knew she was sick, and everyone around her was worried. We couldn't play together any more. When I did get to see her, I had to wear a mask, sanitise my hands. I felt so powerless. I was just a kid, and all I could think was, I want to save her. And then, anyone like her. When Dad got sick, I was struck by that same sense. I want to make a difference.'

He leaned forward then, his palm cupping her cheek, eyes locked to hers in a way that made her pulse trip. 'I have no doubt you will, *cara*.'

Her smile was shy, his praise so heart-warming. It wasn't as if she needed external validation—she knew she had the grades to get into medicine—it was only because of life circumstances that she'd had to put it on hold. But having his support was like a shot in the arm, regardless.

'You're very smart,' he said, after a beat, the praise glowing inside her. She knew it was true, though. Her grades had always been excellent, but hearing it from Massimiliano set her pulse alight. 'I don't think I was expecting you to be so well read, so interesting.'

She pulled a face. 'I think you meant that as a compliment, but I'm not so sure.'

'I mean because you are young. Working in a diner.'

She rolled her eyes, missing the way his mouth quirked in an appreciative smile.

'I always did very well at school,' she said. 'I got a scholarship to study medicine, aced my pre-admission test. But then, he got sick.' She cleared her throat, wishing she didn't still feel that acid reflux when she thought of her dad. 'And while he was sick, I would read the papers to him, every day. He would close his eyes and listen, but if I thought he'd drifted off, and stopped, he'd reach out and squeeze my arm, wanting me to keep going. I would read them back to front for him.'

The sympathy in his expression was impossible to miss. It hit her right in the solar plexus.

'And you haven't heard from your mother since she left?' he asked, gently, settling back in the hot tub, but keeping their legs entwined.

'Not a single card. I have no idea if she's alive or dead.'

His brows knitted together. 'You could hire a detective.'

She rejected that thought. 'Either way, she's dead to me. If she doesn't want to be in my life, why would I push that?'

His eyes raked her face, then, slowly, he nodded. 'I feel the same.'

'About your father.'

He shifted his head in agreement.

'With your father, he'd actually committed crimes. So I presume police were searching for him.'

'There was a massive operation. He has evaded discovery. We know only that he transferred hundreds of millions of euros offshore, money he convinced every single person we knew to invest with him. He must have been planning it for a long time—the detail was meticulous.'

Amelia shook her head. 'But your family was already wealthy. Why do that?'

'We were wealthy enough, but not like this.' He gestured to the view. 'Although, sometimes I think it wasn't about the money at all, so much as the thrill of it. He scammed his friends, he got away with it.'

'But he lost you and your grandfather and ruined your life in the process.'

He made a gruff noise of agreement. 'What he did was also, in all likelihood, the making of me.'

'How so?'

'I was always driven, I suppose, but not like this. From the moment his crimes were revealed, I vowed to repair the damage. To earn enough to pay back every last cent, and then to have enough money that, no matter what my father had done, people would respect us. I didn't realise how entrenched those prejudices would become. The name Moretti remained mud, no matter how much money I had.'

'That's not true,' she disputed. 'You are hugely admired. You're one of the richest men in the world. Your business success is legendary.'

'I am talking about a very specific legacy. The Moretti name, here in Italy and in Europe, the respect that was once afforded us simply because of the generations that have gone before.'

'I thought you didn't care about that.'

'I don't. Either way, the name ends with me, so why do

I care what the value of it is? But my grandfather cares. It is, I suppose you could say, his dying wish.'

Something thudded in her chest. 'You mean the name ends with you because you don't intend to have children?'

His eyes held hers. *'Sì.'*

A shiver ran the length of her spine. 'Does your grandfather know?'

Those dark eyes continued to probe hers, as though looking through her. 'On the contrary, he now feels that children are imminent.'

Comprehension began to dawn. 'Because of our marriage.'

'Yes.'

'Another benefit of pretending this is real,' she murmured.

'A definite advantage.'

'But what happens when we split up?'

Massimiliano's features tightened. 'The future is uncertain, for my grandfather.'

'Yeah,' she said, softly. 'I get that. You don't know how long you'll have him for. But the best-case scenario is that he fights and wins, right? So…isn't that going to destroy him, when we get divorced?'

'I'll cross that bridge when I get to it.'

'You really don't plan on ever having kids?'

'No.' He said it so swiftly, so assuredly, that she knew there was absolutely no wiggle room in his mind.

She bit into her lower lip. 'I'm the opposite. I haven't had the chance to really meet anyone, or date, and I want to achieve a lot professionally before I even think of settling down like that. But I've always known that I would want a family one day.'

He pulled a face, evidently as surprised by her revelation as she had been his. 'It's not for me.'

She moved even closer, a thrill of adrenaline firing in her veins. 'I'm completely alone, Massimiliano. Even before my dad passed away, I was lonely. It was just the two of us. I wasn't enough for him and he wasn't enough for me, even though we both tried to be. And now, he's gone, and I have this big, yawning chasm in here.' She pressed her fingers between her breasts. 'I want to love and be loved, even when I'm terrified of how vulnerable that will make me. I want to know what it's like to live in a happy family, to be surrounded by kids, who aren't just a part of me, but a part of each other, too. Who are one another's best friends, no matter what.'

His eyes flicked over her face. 'Because you never had that.'

She nodded once.

'Funny,' he remarked, wrapping his arms around her waist, holding her tight to his body. 'You and I lived such similar lives, in some ways, and yet we both want the complete opposite now.'

'I don't think it's funny,' she said, shaking her head. 'I think it's just a function of who we are. You crave control and limits in all things. I crave connection.' She lifted her shoulders. 'We're just different.'

'And yet, we work.'

Her smile was bright, but inside, she felt a strange flipping in her chest. 'That's because there's something in this for both of us. Connection for me, in the here and now. Control for you, in the knowledge that it's time-limited. Everyone wins.'

'*Sì, carina.* Everyone wins.'

And as Amelia leaned forward to press her lips to Massimiliano's, she was conscious of the stars twinkling brightly overhead, the beauty of the city in the background, her gladness that they still had almost two years left in this marriage. While it might have been temporary, it was the closest thing to perfect Amelia had ever known, and she was going to make the most of every second.

A month later, Massimiliano found himself reflecting on the new routine he'd slipped into. A routine that was nothing like his usual life. Once upon a time, before Amelia, he'd worked long days, staying at his desk until late in the night, travelling often. Now he left work when his staff did, eager to get home and see his wife. While she was his wife.

Because their deal was for two years, and he had no intention of extending that. Why would he? It had been six weeks of marriage and, while he still felt as infatuated with her as ever before, he was quietly confident that wouldn't last.

And yet, there was something about her that constantly pulled the rug out from under him.

Case in point: when he walked into his apartment that night, it was to find the lights off, and a warm glow coming from the living room. Bemused, he strode deeper and laughed when he saw that she'd strung fairy lights from one side of the room to the other. The fire was lit, and, in front of it, she'd erected what looked to be a teepee.

'What on earth is going on?' he asked, looking around in time to see a smiling Amelia padding out of the kitchen, barefoot, and wearing one of his button-down shirts, undone to between her breasts, so he felt an immediate kick of desire. To hell with whatever this was: he wanted to take her to bed, then and there. Or the sofa. The floor. Anywhere.

'Promise you won't laugh?' she asked, lips twisting to the side as she stopped frustratingly out of reach and began to swirl her wedding ring.

He dipped his head, silently agreeing but making no such verbal promise. He'd never known anyone like her.

'So, this is a bit of a tradition,' she said, gesturing towards the teepee.

'Okay, I'm listening.'

'It's this thing my dad would do every year. We didn't have money, as you know. We couldn't afford to go on holidays or anything, even camping. But he loved to camp. So he'd do this for me, each year.'

'For you?'

She cleared her throat. 'For my birthday.'

He felt the bottom drop out of his stomach as, inwardly, he smothered a curse. Her birthday? He should have known. He'd had her paperwork, for their wedding. That would have clearly shown the relevant date. Why hadn't he made a note of that?

Because he'd had no expectation of her becoming any part of his life. She'd been just a convenient bride, a chess piece to manoeuvre into position, nothing more.

'I should have known.'

'Not at all,' she said, shaking her head. 'I didn't mention it. I wouldn't have wanted you to make a fuss, or do anything different from this.' Then she stepped forward, and pressed her hand to his. 'Last year, Dad was really sick, but he still made me set it all up, and wheel him into the lounge room,' she said, her smile so heartbreakingly sad that he felt himself being torn to shreds. 'And I remember sitting there thinking it would be the last year that I'd ever do this. Because it's too sad to do it on my own,' she added, lips tugging to the side again. 'And the thing is, it just feels right to share it with you. I don't know why. Is that stupid?'

He stared down at her, fiercely ignoring the twisting in his gut, the heating in his chest, and shook his head. 'It's as far from stupid as you can get.' He cupped her face, holding her still, his voice thick as he said, 'Happy birthday, Signora Moretti. I'm glad we can do this together.'

The next day, Massimiliano's assistant called Amelia around the time she was starting to expect him home. '*Signora*, Signor Moretti has asked if you can be available to be picked up in an hour's time.'

Amelia frowned. 'I can be, yes. What for?'

There was a pause. 'He asked for it to be a surprise.'

Amelia's cheeks hurt from the force of her smile as she said, 'Okay, tell him I'll see him soon.'

She had no idea what he had planned, so hedged her bets by dressing in a pair of sleek black trousers and a cashmere sweater, which she teamed with champagne-coloured leather flats and a clutch bag. Precisely one hour after the call, the discreet buzzer rang. With anticipation firing her insides, she slipped out, and took the elevator to the elegant, high-security foyer. A black limousine was parked beyond the glass doors. She walked quietly over the tiles, and out into the cold afternoon air. It was midway through autumn. Winter was approaching, and, with it, the promise of Christmas, the feeling of change as a new year came. A new year that took her deeper into this marriage, and closer to the end of it.

She pushed that thought aside, not wanting it to darken her mood, or this moment.

Massimiliano's driver stood with the limousine door open and she held her breath as she stepped in, eyes sweeping the car for her husband, only to be disappointed. While he wasn't there, on the seat opposite, there was a present, with a Post-it note that said, 'open me'.

She clicked her seat belt in place and reached for the present as the car pulled out of the driveway. She slid it from the bag, and unwrapped it quickly. It was a book, very, very old, and written completely in Italian, though that didn't matter. A gentle flick through the aged pages showed it for what it was: a record of the most prominent families of Europe, dating back centuries. He'd bookmarked two pages. The Rossis, and the Morettis.

She sat back in the seat, smiling to herself, as the car weaved through a twilight-covered Rome, thinking how much she liked the idea of their families being linked in this book. Though she infinitely preferred the fact they were linked in marriage. *Even when it was fake,* a voice in her mind sternly reminded her, and just in the nick of time, too.

First a private jet, and now a helicopter, she thought, with a quirk of her lips, as she stepped into the beautiful, sleek aircraft and fastened the seat belt. Still no sign of Massimiliano, but here, there was yet another gift. She reached for it as the rotor blades began to spin, and with the deafening noise that accompanied their lift-off, she focused not on their altitude but rather the unwrapping of the present. It was a box, the sort that would be perfect for a necklace, so as she clicked it open, she fully expected it to be some kind of jewellery. And in a sense, it was, she supposed, but it was also so much more. For inside the box was a case, and in that case was the most beautifully stunning personalised stethoscope she could possibly imagine. Gold-plated and engraved with 'Dr Redgrave', it was both perfect, and heartbreaking. Because there, in delicate cursive script, was a name that she now found utterly jarring. The name she'd used all her life—a rejection of her mother's surname—now didn't seem to fit her at all. At least, it fitted only part of her.

Mostly, though, it was such a graphic display of what they'd agreed to: that this marriage would last only two years. That she'd be divorced, and single, when she graduated from her degree, and began treating patients.

She brushed her finger over the engraving as the helicopter flew across Rome, and towards the south. She didn't know if it was because she wanted to erase it, or to commit the name to memory, to remind herself of who she really was. For all that she'd come to feel like Massimiliano's wife, it wasn't real. None of this was.

Her heart slammed against her ribs when she disembarked from the helicopter and saw what he'd done. She had no idea where she was—a winery, somewhere, going by the rows of vines she could see from the clearing. But here, there was a large patch of lawn, and in the middle of it, with a view of the gently rolling hills, was a large tent. And candles. Candles everywhere, far enough from where the helicopter had set down that the rotor blades hadn't affected their flickering, glowing warmth. There was also, just a few metres away, Massimiliano Moretti. Her husband in name only. Her husband, in her heart.

She knew it as soon as she saw him. It was the stethoscope that had done it. The beautiful gift, so thoughtful, that was everything she might have wanted, were it not for the engraving. Reminding her of who she would be, after this. Who she'd been before him.

She didn't want to be Amelia Redgrave again. She wanted to be Amelia Moretti, for as long as they both should live.

She wanted this to be real.

She wanted, in short, the impossible. Because no matter what had happened between them, Massimiliano had been perfectly clear, all the way along. He didn't want marriage. He didn't want children. This was temporary for him. Never mind that it was great. That they worked. They worked because they each respected the other's needs.

Her emotions were a painful jumble, pulling her from one direction to the other.

Because a part of her couldn't help wondering: what if he'd changed, too? What if he wanted more, too? This evening, after all, was *not* the act of a business partner, or faux husband.

Pulse thumping, she walked quickly away from the helicopter, towards Massimiliano.

'Doctor,' he murmured as he pulled her close.

'Nowhere near yet,' she said, the words more clipped than she'd intended, so she forced an over-bright smile. 'This is amazing.' The praise was drawn from deep within.

'I'm very grateful you shared your birthday tradition with me last night, but I thought, tonight, you might like to partake in the real thing.'

Her heart turned over. The real thing. Not fake. Not a dupe, like her ring, and their marriage, but genuine, everlasting love. She could no longer deny it: that was what she desperately wanted. More than anything in the world. More than the career she'd always thought she wanted, that now felt so much less urgent, more than the life she'd planned for, more than anything. She would give it all up, if it meant she could stay here, with Massimiliano.

Heaven help her, she was completely lost.

CHAPTER THIRTEEN

'WHERE ARE WE, ANYWAY?' she said, much later that night, as they lay on a softer-than-clouds mattress, looking up into the night sky, naked limbs entwined, covered in a fine sheen of perspiration despite the cool night.

'A winery in Frascati.'

She looked around at the silhouette of vines, now coated in milky moonlight. 'Why here?'

'Because the stars are never clearer than here,' he said. 'And because it's private.'

She blinked up at him. 'Is it yours?'

'Of course.'

She bit back a smile at that. His confidence bordering on arrogance was so typically him. Her skin lifted in goosebumps as her soul recognised its pair, its partner, and her skin flushed all over.

'I still can't believe you did this.'

'Can't you?' he asked, eyes roaming her face and practically jump-starting her heart. 'Why is that?'

'You just don't seem like someone who would go to this kind of trouble.'

He reached out and touched a finger to her chin, gently angling her face to his. 'You deserve good things, Amelia. You've fought hard, for too long. If nothing else, I'm glad this marriage has given you the freedom to live whatever life you choose.'

It was as though the weight of every atom in the universe were pressing down against her chest, making it almost impossible to breathe. To think. To weigh up the risks of what she now knew she must do.

'I have to ask you something,' she said, twisting her engagement ring between the fingers on either side of it, so his eyes glanced down at the ring before zipping back to her face.

Giving her vital seconds to rethink this.

But the weight on her chest made it impossible.

She had to know.

She'd always faced everything in life head-on. She was not someone to run and hide, nor bury her head in the sand. She was a fighter, and now she had to fight for her marriage.

If there was any chance he might feel for her as she did for him, she had to know. Because all of a sudden, not having said this aloud was suffocating her.

'I have to ask you something,' she repeated, because there was really no choice about it.

'You said that already.'

She bit into her lower lip. 'A few weeks ago, you told me that we were different in a vital way.'

His brow furrowed, as though he didn't remember.

'We were in the hot tub, talking about…' she faltered slightly, gaze dropping to his chest, before lifting back to his lips, then his eyes '…marriage. Children.'

'Ah, yes,' he said quietly. 'I remember.'

'You said that you've known for a long time you don't want marriage and kids. That your mind is made up.'

'*Sì.*'

Her belly hurt, but she was a fighter, and the fight wasn't over. 'I guess I'm wondering how firmly made up your mind is. Like, is there any part of you that thinks maybe you're wrong?'

In the same way she would have felt a change in the weather, a shift in the wind's direction, she felt the change in Massimiliano. The slight tension in his arms, the look in his face.

'No,' he said, after an infinitesimal pause. 'Not even the smallest part of me wonders that.'

She closed her eyes in the most instinctive reaction to his statement that her body could muster.

'Why do you ask?' The question seemed almost to be dragged from him against his will.

Because he knew. She could tell, he knew.

'It doesn't matter,' she murmured. Apparently, she wasn't a fighter, after all.

'If it matters to you, then you can say,' he offered. But she knew he didn't want to hear. And she didn't want to burden him with her admission. That she'd fallen in love with him was her mistake. Her stupidity. He'd warned her all along to take care—she just hadn't known how. And now she alone would live with the consequences of that.

He put up with it for a week. For a whole week after that night at his Frascati vineyard, he went through the motions of their marriage with the clarity of what she hadn't said.

That she loved him. Or thought she did.

He watched his convenient bride, his *contessina*, act her part to perfection. Having dinner with his grandfather, then her grandparents, smiling at him as though her heart weren't breaking when he could see, so clearly, that it was.

Because he knew her.

He knew her every impulse, instinct, thought and feeling. He knew her heart, her soul, her mind, her dreams. He knew and understood her.

He had known, even in London, that she was special and unique. He'd also known that she was innocent and inexperienced, that there was a risk of her wanting more than he could offer. A risk of her thinking she was in love with him. He'd known, and failed to protect her. He'd taken what he wanted—her body—and destroyed her heart in the process. And it couldn't go on any longer.

He wouldn't allow it to.

'Amelia?' he called, scanning the apartment for her before he could back out of doing the right thing, simply because it felt so good having her here. 'We need to talk.'

'That sounds ominous,' she said, keeping her voice neutral, acting the part of the carefree fake wife he wanted. She was midway through stepping into the dress she was wearing to dinner. She pulled it in place and zipped it up, sucking in a deep breath as she waited.

But Massimiliano didn't play his part in return. They'd long ago abandoned separate bedrooms and now lived in his; and his face, when he stalked into the room, was like a thunderclap. She blinked in surprise, pushing down the worry that was churning inside her.

'We need to talk,' he repeated.

She tilted her head to the side, not sure she could trust herself to say anything in return.

'I have good news.' His smile didn't reach his eyes.

Something held her impossibly, completely still. 'Oh?'

'I've realised something important. We've done what we set out to achieve, with this marriage.'

Her heart stopped beating. 'Have we?' The words were barely a whisper.

'My grandfather is euphoric. He's been inundated with invitations by his so-called, one-time friends. You've met your grandparents. I don't think there's any need to keep going with this charade.'

She flinched. *Charade?*

She shook her head slightly. 'I'm sorry. What does that mean?'

He let out a sigh. 'I can't be responsible for you not pursuing your dreams, Amelia. Studying medicine at your age is going to require you to start as soon as possible. I've organised everything. An apartment for you in London, a tutor for your UCAT; naturally I'll pay the fees.'

It felt as though a knife were plunging into her side. 'What?'

He moved closer then, so they were standing toe to toe. 'You shouldn't have to put off your life. You deserve so much better.'

She deserved *him*. That was all she wanted.

'I don't understand. What about…two years? I thought we had two years.'

A muscle jerked in his jaw. 'You need to leave.' For the briefest moment, the mask slipped. He sounded emotional. Conflicted.

As though he didn't really want this.

'If there's an occasion that requires you, in that time, you can come back. We can stay legally married for the duration.'

She shook her head, his words making absolutely no sense.

'This isn't really about my degree,' she surmised, seeing through that easily.

He closed his eyes, nostrils flaring. 'You need to go.'

She blinked quickly, to clear the tears. 'Why?'

He looked at her then, eyes piercing her soul. 'Because I think you've fallen in love with me. Or believe you have, anyway.'

She staggered backwards.

'And I can't keep you here, seeing you suffer like this. Seeing you suffer through every dinner, every night, every kiss, every touch. I will not be the reason you are hurting.'

She flinched and felt her heart burst at the same time. She blinked away quickly, focusing on the view of Rome exposed through his bedroom windows.

'I—don't—'

He gripped her upper arms, so her gaze was wrenched back to his. 'Do you love me?'

She opened her mouth to deny it, but how could she? That would be the worst betrayal she could possibly know. Defiantly, she tilted her chin, meeting his gaze unflinchingly. 'Yes,' she said, because he deserved to know. 'Yes,' she repeated, because he *had* to know. Because that reality was bursting through her in glorious Technicolor, just as the whole world had been after their first time together. 'I love you, Massimiliano Moretti, and if I had my way, I would stay here in Italy, for ever and always, as your wife. Not just in name, but in both of our hearts.' She pressed her hand to his chest, feeling the way it was beating, hard, against his ribs.

His skin paled, as though it was the worst thing he could have heard.

'Amelia,' he murmured softly. 'That wasn't our deal.'

Their deal seemed like something two strangers had made, a thousand years ago.

'My turn to ask the questions,' she said, lifting her hand to his lips and pressing it there. He stayed silent, even when that was not in his nature. 'Have you ever felt this way about a woman? Have you ever been with someone as long as you have me?'

'Our marriage is not real.'

'No, but this is,' she said, brushing her other hand behind his back, and holding him close.

'Sex,' he muttered.

But she denied that quickly, too. 'Not just sex, and we both know it.'

A muscle jerked in his jaw as she stared at him, half daring him to contradict her. To his credit, he didn't.

'I realised something, a few weeks ago,' she said. 'I was a virgin, when I met you, but in some ways, you were too. When have you ever made love to a woman you had feelings for? When has it ever been more than sex for you?'

He stared down at her, as if silently begging her to stop.

'Am I the only woman?'

'No,' he said, surprising her. No, damn near knocking her sideways. 'I was engaged once before.'

She felt the world lurching beneath her feet. 'What?'

'Many years ago. It was a mistake. But at the time, I thought I loved her.'

Amelia felt it like a body blow. She shook her head, as if that could dispel his words, and the awful cloud of jealousy that was permeating her spirit and soul. 'When?' she asked, finding it almost impossible to believe he'd kept this from her.

'Before my father left. We were young. Her parents were strict—they expected my commitment. So, I proposed. But when my father's scandal broke, she dropped me faster than you can imagine. I believed we were in love, but it was a mistake.'

'That's so shallow,' she said, angrily. 'To desert you when you needed her most.'

'I didn't need her, though. I was wrong. About her, us, about our future.' He cupped her face, then, his expression earnest. 'Just as you're wrong now.'

'No,' she denied, quickly.

'I'm not the man for you.'

'How can you say that?'

He ground his jaw. 'Because I will never be able to give you what you want, what you deserve.'

'What if all I want is you?'

'I'm not available.'

'But you are,' she said, surprised when a sob burst from her. She hadn't realised how close she was to crying. 'Can't you see that? You have shared yourself with me, ever since we met, and I have loved every single piece of you. Doesn't that mean anything?'

He shook his head once, his jaw tight. His whole body tight. As if he was holding himself together with the force of iron.

'Massimiliano?'

'*Fu-u-uck,*' he groaned. 'Stop.'

'I don't understand.'

'You know how I always said you could ask me to

stop, any time? That you needed to have that safe word? That boundary? Well, *this* is my boundary. I'm asking you to stop.'

'Why?' she pushed, certain she was getting close to something real and raw. Something he didn't want to express. Something that mattered, deeply.

'Because you're asking for the impossible.'

'Does it feel impossible? Does anything about us seem out of reach? Or is it everything we deserve?'

He ground his jaw. 'It's never going to happen.'

'Why not?'

'I told you—'

'Just tell me *why*,' she pleaded. 'If you're going to bloody pack me away like some box, send me back to England, at least have the courtesy of explaining to me why you won't even give this—*us*—a chance. A real chance.'

His eyes bored into hers, and she saw the plea in their depths, the visible sign that he was done with this conversation. She loved him. She loved him completely, with all of her heart, so, on the one hand, she was tempted to let him off the hook. To accept his plans without arguing. But she loved their relationship even more, and their future was one worth fighting for.

'I didn't have you pegged as a coward.'

His eyes flashed with emotions she didn't comprehend, and she relished that. She knew she might have been pushing her finger hard into whatever emotional bruises he carried, but she didn't—couldn't—care. She had her own bruises, and right now he was hurting each and every one of them.

'Don't,' he said, closing his eyes.

'What's wrong? Too scared to have this conversation?'

'Yes,' he said, opening his eyes there, surprising her with the intensity of his gaze. 'You're right. I'm a coward. Does that make you happy, Amelia? Is that what you want to hear?'

It wasn't. It hurt her. It hurt her to see him face up to his own vulnerabilities, to cloak himself in that weakness.

'I need you to go,' he said, the words ground out, heavy and dark. 'I will not let you love me. I will not let you stay here, offering me that, all the while knowing that at any point, on a whim, you can take it away again. And I will sure as hell never let myself love you.'

There was so much emotion in his words. So much feeling, and past hurt. She ached for him. For the people he'd once loved, who'd turned their backs on him. His fiancée, the society crowd he'd considered friends, and, worst of all, his own father.

'I don't know if there's anyone else on earth who would understand why you feel that way as perfectly as I do.' She moved forward again, wrapping her arms around his waist, looking up into his face. 'There is a specific emptiness that comes from being abandoned by your parents. A hole in your chest that opens up when you have to accept that one of the two people who should have been biologically hard-wired to love you has let you down so catastrophically.' She lifted one hand to stroke his stubbled jaw. 'But from the moment I met you, that hole has started to zip closed. Parts of me I thought would be for ever empty are all full up, because of you. Tell me it's not the same. Tell me you don't feel that, too.'

His nostrils flared as he expelled a breath. Fierce and sharp, full of rejection. 'You are unlike anyone I've ever known,' he said, finally, but even then, the words were laced with a dark anger. 'If anyone was going to make me forget, it would be you. But I have lived with this a long time. Longer than you can image. I will never allow love to weaken me again, *cara*. Not for you, not for anyone. If you love me, if you understand me, then you'll know I'm telling the truth.'

Another sob bubbled up inside her then, because he was right. He was being honest, and she knew that. In a million years, Massimiliano Moretti would never change. Not for her, nor for anyone, just as he'd said.

'I'll organise a car to take you to the airport.'

'Don't tell me what to do, where to go.'

'It's your life,' he pointed out.

But she rejected that, with a deep sense of despair. Since she was a little girl, she'd had one clear idea of what she wanted. To be a doctor; to make people better. But how much of that came from trauma? How much of her aspiration was really the result of a little girl who'd known loss and felt powerless to help?

And then, she'd met Massimiliano, and parts of her had healed without her realising it, so she wondered if what really needed fixing, all this time, was herself. It didn't mean she wouldn't pursue medicine, it just meant it was no longer the sole aspiration in her life. It no longer felt like her purpose for being.

Because there was Massimiliano as well, and this marriage they'd been creating. But was it all a fake? Was he right?

She shook her head, silently rejecting that, but her fingers toyed with the ring she wore and a lightning bolt of clarity split through her.

'It's all fake to you,' she whispered, blinking across at

him. 'Just like this.' She slid the cut-glass ring from her finger and held it out towards him.

He shook his head once. 'Please, keep it.'

'I don't want it.'

'Keep it, in case we need—'

'To keep fooling everyone?' she said, in a manic sense of disbelief. Even then, he was being pragmatic, thinking about their fake marriage. He was letting her go, but still clinging to the idea of this. The charade, as he'd called it.

'Fine.' She pushed it onto her finger as her stomach rolled with pain.

'I never wanted to hurt you,' he said, quietly. 'This was not my plan.'

'Yeah, well, life doesn't always go according to plan, Massimiliano.'

'I'm aware of that.'

'You just have to roll with it. So what if this turned out to be more than either of us expected? So what if we fell in love—'

'That's not—' He cut himself off with a curse, then strode across the room, pulling her into his arms. 'That's not what this is.' And he kissed her, hard, passionately, his body melding to hers, big and strong, so her insides hammered and her heart thumped hard to her ribs. Her hands curved around his back on autopilot, and she tasted salt in her mouth from the tears that were in freefall.

'That,' he said, pulling up from her, 'is what you're mistaking for love.'

She shook her head quickly.

'You have never been with a man. You are overwhelmed by the sex, nothing more.'

'How dare you?' she spat, pushing him away then,

stepping back at the same time. 'Don't tell me what I feel. Don't tell me I'm not smart enough to know the difference between sex and love.'

'With all due respect, how could you have any idea?'

Her lips parted on a rush of air.

'You have been so starved of love, you are desperate to find it here, now, with me,' he said, cutting her deep. Because on the one hand, he was right. Her mother's desertion had starved her of maternal love, and then her father's death had left her completely alone. But he was also wrong, because, before that, her father had adored her, and she'd known the uncomplicated sense of security that came from understanding herself to be safe in someone's heart space.

'I was right before,' she whispered. 'You are such a coward. Not only do you refuse to admit how you feel, you can't face up to the reality of what *I* feel, and, worse, you're using what you know of my life against me, trying to make out I'm some damaged little orphan that couldn't possibly know real love.' She sucked in a ragged breath. 'Well, you can try to make yourself feel better by saying I'm misreading what I feel, but you're wrong. You're so damned wrong. This is love. All-consuming, heart-filling love.' She stalked back towards him then, jabbing a finger in his chest. 'And whatever happens in your life, when you're old and lonely and thinking about things, I hope you look back on this night and realise you had a chance to do something real and meaningful. That you had a chance to live a life that was full of significance and love, but that you were too scared. I hope you feel the weight of this decision for the rest of your goddamned life, Massimiliano, because letting me go is the biggest mistake you'll ever make.'

And she stalked out of their room, dashing away her tears as she looked around blindly for her handbag.

'Where are you going?' he asked, right behind her, voice satisfyingly raw and husky.

'That's none of your business.'

'You are still my wife.'

She whirled around then, fury spreading through her. 'Don't be such a jerk. I'm not your wife, any more than I am a doctor. Wanting something doesn't make it happen.'

His jaw shifted as he ground his teeth. 'You are my wife, to the rest of the world. Wherever you go, you are under my protection.'

'You've made me wealthy,' she pointed out. 'I can hire my own damned security, Massimiliano. I don't need anything from you,' she said, tilting her chin defiantly. 'Except the one thing you'll clearly never give me.'

'You are acting like a child.'

She glared at him. 'And you're acting like an asshole. I know which one I'd rather be.'

She stalked to the door and wrenched it inwards.

'At least take my car—'

She sent him a withering look. 'I want *nothing* from you. Got it?'

CHAPTER FOURTEEN

He had his security follow her cab. If she was going to be delusional about the very real risks her public profile presented, then that was her choice. But for Massimiliano's part, protecting her was now a requirement. He'd created this situation. There was no way he'd let harm befall her because he'd failed to care for her.

His conscience was already groaning under the weight of their argument, her accusations. His mind reeling with accusations she'd made that he didn't want to address, sentiments that were swallowed into the 'no-go' segment of his brain, protecting him from analysing them further.

Amelia went to a hotel in the city. Once he had the name, he called and made sure the room was charged to him. While she was right—he'd settled a decent amount on her—he didn't want her using her money for a situation that was his creation. He also sent a security team to stay at the hotel, to wait in the foyer in shifts, so they could accompany her when she went out. He needed to know she was safe.

The next day, he had her clothes and accessories packaged up and sent to the hotel. He'd thought of doing it himself, but the moment his hand had glanced across one of her silk dresses, and he remembered her wearing it, he'd stalked out of the wardrobe and outsourced the task instead. A glimpse into the fantasy life they'd had threatened to rock his certainty that he'd done the right thing.

He'd partly been expecting some acknowledgement of the clothes, though. A text, a call.

And he'd craved that. He missed her like hell. Only the knowledge that he'd done what was right kept him from calling her himself.

Just to hear her voice.

The third day after she left, she texted.

Seriously, this is stalking. Get your security guys to go away.

He frowned. Why couldn't she be reasonable? How could she fail to see his duty was to protect her, no matter what?

Are they bothering you?

He waited, gut churning, as he stared at his phone, hoping she'd say something back. Anything.

The next day, he got another text.

Massimiliano, you cannot ride roughshod over my wishes. I'm a big girl. I'm prepared to take the risk of being on my own. Call off your team.

And when they were still guarding her the next day:

If you respect me, even one iota, you will do as I say. I'm a grown woman. I can make my own decisions.

He replied:

This is a mistake. You're vulnerable.

It's my mistake to make.

Just as letting her go had been his mistake to make, according to Amelia.

He drummed his fingers against his knee, torn between what he knew was right and what she was asking of him. Torn, even when he knew he'd have to do as she asked. Because Amelia was right. This was her life, and he'd more or less opted out of it.

Except, he hadn't.

There was no one on earth he was more invested in. No one on earth he cared for more. It was simply that his caring had to be from a distance. He wanted to know she was safe, comfortable, and achieving her dreams, even when he would never be a part of any of it. It was impossible to explain, or rationalise, but, from the sidelines, he knew he'd always be her biggest champion. Or he would have been, if she'd let him.

It was the worst month of Amelia's life—which was saying a lot. She'd been through so much in her twenty-four years, and somehow, walking out on her husband, knowing he would rather keep his head in the sand and be alone than admit he loved her, too, was a special form of torment.

She stayed at the hotel, uncaring for the cost. He'd given her a small fortune, but she'd chosen a modest room, and it was a little off the tourist track, so it was quiet.

She kept to herself. It was one of the reasons the guards weren't needed.

Weeks passed, in which she didn't leave her room, except once, to see her grandparents. When they asked about Massimiliano, she smiled a brittle smile and forced herself to lie. They were overjoyed, and shocked because Massimiliano had taken over their business affairs, and promised to make everything better. Her heart twisted at that. It was just as he'd promised.

When they asked her and Massimiliano to join them for a celebratory dinner, she demurred. She couldn't face being in the same room with him. But after a month, and several invitations, when they insisted on both Massimiliano and her joining them for a charity gala, she knew she had to see them at some point.

'I don't know if Massimiliano can make it,' she said. 'But I'll come with you, if you don't mind me third-wheeling.'

They didn't understand the expression and she was too tired to explain it to them. She was fatigued all over. Exhausted, body and soul. It took her for ever to get ready for the event. She'd been hermiting away in her hotel room for so long, her nails were bare, her hair lank, her skin pale. But she set about glamming herself up as best she was able, styling her hair, applying make-up carefully, choosing a dress she'd adored when she'd tried it on back in London, in what felt like another life.

It was only when she pulled the dress on that she realised how much weight she'd lost. Where once it had fitted her like a glove, it was now loose all over. She frowned, studying her reflection, and deciding it still looked passably elegant. She chose a pair of sky-high stilettos and a matching clutch, then made her way to the door of her room.

But when she touched the handle to leave, she was hit by a wave of panic. Exhaustion. Dread.

She couldn't do this.

She couldn't go out and see people, pretend she was fine, act as though everything were normal. Her gaze dropped to her ring, the copycat version she'd had him make, rather than wear the stunning Moretti diamond. Fake. Just like them.

But her heart quivered at even the thought of that, because they were *not* fake. He'd been so wrong that night. When she'd left his stunning penthouse, she'd been spitting-chips mad, but she'd still harboured some hopes that he'd come to his senses. That a few days apart would make him realise what he'd had—and lost. But the next day, he'd rubbed salt in the wound by sending her clothes over. She'd wanted to torch them all, but had kept them partly out of necessity, partly out of sentimentality. On the few times she'd left the hotel, trying to act normal, to convince herself she'd be okay—just as she had after her dad's death—she'd seen his bloody security guards and wanted to snap something.

She didn't need his damn overprotective concern. She needed him.

The security guards had gone, finally, but Amelia had barely left her room.

And even now, with her grandparents expecting to meet her at this ritzy event, she couldn't do it. She couldn't open the door, let alone step through it.

She sobbed, pressing her back against the wall, dropping her head into her hands and giving into the grief.

Letting it overtake her completely, before shuffling back to bed and lying down. She typed out a quick apology message to her grandparents, before curling up in the foetal position and doing her best to blot out the world.

At first, he told himself he was glad she'd left. Glad she'd listened to him, finally, and let him send her away. He hadn't been able to give her love, but at least he'd given her freedom. True freedom—including financial. And the hope of a future with someone better.

Only, he couldn't think of that. He couldn't think of another man in her life, touching her, kissing her, listening to her laugh, hearing her stories, watching her succeed, as Massimiliano knew she would. Because Amelia Redgrave was a rare diamond. A gem more valuable than any other in existence.

So why couldn't he do what she'd asked, and try this? Why couldn't he try to make this work? The pain in her features, etched there by his rejection, had been unbearable to see. He'd wanted to pull her into his arms and give her *anything* in that moment.

But he knew himself.

It would never work.

His past had shaped him. In many ways, it had made him strong. Unbreakable. But only because he refused to rely on anyone. He was his own person, with impenetrable walls around every part of himself—most vitally, his heart.

It had been his approach to all things, for almost as long as he could remember. At nineteen, his entire world had splintered into shards around him, piercing him with the shock of rejection, the suspicion of his involvement, the shame of his father, the scandal, accepting that his father had knowingly thrown him into this life, and apparently not cared.

Every day since, his father's absence had been like a blade in his chest. He'd learned to live with that, to walk side by side with the pain, but that wasn't the same thing as not feeling it. His father was likely still out there, living his life, as though he hadn't left a father and son behind to clean up the mess. To face the consequences.

It had taken ruthless determination and unfailing strength of mind to do what Massimiliano had. To rebuild their fortune, repay his father's debts, and then to turn their modest family empire into what it was today: a world leader in so many industries.

That had always been enough for him. This life of his, independent of all people, of feeling, of caring about anyone besides his grandfather, had been his solace. He had everything he needed. Sex when he wanted it had always been easy enough to obtain, and to walk away from. So while he felt, at present, as though a part of him had been ripped out with Amelia's departure a month earlier, he also knew it would eventually pass. At his core, Massimiliano was heartless—he'd let his heart fade to nothing many years ago, and he told himself he was still glad. Or he would be, when he stopped thinking of Amelia so damned much, and missing her like hell.

The call came through while he was still at his desk. Bleary-eyed, he reached for his phone, checking the time displayed on his laptop screen with a scowl. Nine o'clock. He'd been at his office since…he couldn't remember. Days? He glanced down at his suit, rubbed a hand over his stubbled jaw, before swiping the call to answer. He pinned the phone between his ear and shoulder as he extended his hand for a glass of Scotch.

'Massimiliano,' he said.

'Massi, it's me.'

His grandfather's voice had him closing his eyes, his gut rolling with regret. He'd barely seen the old man since Amelia had left. He hadn't wanted to go through the motions of faking their marriage, even when it was for the old man's sake. He'd hated it. Hated pretending he was fine, talking about Amelia as though…as though what? It hadn't all turned to shit? As though he hadn't broken her heart? As though her leaving hadn't broken him? Broken him into a thousand goddamned pieces, flooding him with a constant sense of…loss.

The worst loss he'd ever known.

She was right about him. He was a coward. He'd lived his life in fear of having someone he cared about turn their back on him. He'd unintentionally—at first—protected himself from ever letting that happen, and then very, very consciously. He'd pushed everyone away, kept people at arm's length as though his life depended on it.

He'd thought the shock of loss, the sense of betrayal, were the worst things, but it turned out it was just…absence. Because he'd controlled this situation with Amelia. He'd ended things with her before she could do that to him. He'd seen the writing on the wall, known that at some point she'd likely leave him, and it would be easier if he could manage the timeline, the circumstances, removing the element of surprise from it all.

It hadn't stung any less.

It had hurt a hell of a lot more, because he woke up

with the guilt of knowing, every single day, that it was his fault. Their misery was on him.

'What's going on with your wife?'

He flinched, his gut rolling.

'Excuse me?'

'She was meant to be at this event tonight. I thought you might come, too. But she told her grandparents she wasn't well, at the last minute. They say they hardly hear from her these days.' He lowered his voice. 'They think she might be pregnant.'

Massimiliano scrunched up his eyes, instantly rejecting that. Or trying to. But the simple, innocent speculation wasn't anathema to him as it should have been. It wasn't offensive or unwelcome.

In a split second, he saw Amelia's stomach growing round with their baby and his whole body surged with a raw, powerful emotion. Possession. Need. *Happiness.*

Intense, all-consuming happiness, so forceful it took his breath away, so he could hardly speak.

'Massi?'

'She's not,' he said, the words choked out as he stood, looking around his office like a man being dragged out of a long coma. 'She's fine, *Nonno*. She's fine.'

'They worry, because of Aria. They don't want to lose Amelia, too.'

He closed his eyes as those words exploded inside him. 'They won't lose her,' he said, with fierce determination.

He disconnected the call without asking his grandfather a single question. He didn't have a second to spare. In the pit of his stomach, he suspected he was already living on borrowed time. Worse? That he'd lost everything, because of his own stupidity, his own cowardice, just as she'd said.

* * *

Amelia tried to ignore the banging at the door. She tried to blot it out. She hadn't ordered room service. She didn't need a cleaning service. She didn't even know what time it was.

But the banging wouldn't stop.

Eventually, smothering a curse, she pushed out of bed and dragged herself down the corridor, feeling as if she had a cement truck weighing her down. Uncaring that her hair was messed up and her make-up undoubtedly smudged, she wrenched in the door, prepared to give vent to all her feelings and drop a furious tirade.

But it wasn't some naughty child playing a hotel version of Ding, Dong, Ditch.

On the other side of her door, just a few feet away, was the man she'd married. Her husband. The word breathed through her before she could block it out.

'Thank God,' he said, not waiting to be invited in. Instead, he pushed past her, his suited sleeve brushing her arm so she shivered at his touch. 'You're still here.'

She blinked at him, frowning, because she didn't understand anything. Why he was here, what he was talking about.

'I'm—what?'

'At the hotel,' he said, jamming his hands in his pockets. 'I knew the room was still being charged, but you could have left. I wasn't sure. I just—'

She blinked. 'What do you mean?'

'The fact the room is still being hired by you is no guarantee that you're using it.'

She shook her head. 'You are making no sense. Where did you think I was?'

'I don't know,' he said, dragging a hand through his hair. 'All I could think, on the drive over here, was that for the last four weeks, I have had no idea about your days. No idea what you've been doing, who you've been seeing. No idea if you're safe, happy, if you're okay.'

She blinked quickly, hating the acid that burned her throat, threatening tears. 'Why do you care?'

He stared at her long and hard, his eyes dark with feeling.

'Because you were right. You were right.' He walked back towards her, standing so close he could touch, but not. Not reaching for her, so her insides twisted with a desire to sway forward and feel him once more.

'What about?'

'This. Us. Everything. Me, and what's holding me back. That I'm a goddamn coward. That I'd prefer to deny myself the pleasure of you, and the life we could share, rather than risk losing you unexpectedly. That I have been hiding my head in the sand my whole adult life, because I didn't want to get hurt. But I am hurt. I am hurt in here,' he said, pushing his hands to his chest. 'I have been hurting every second of every day since you left. Letting you go tore me apart, Amelia.'

His words were like honey on her frazzled nerves, but she shook her head, unwilling to completely trust them. Even when she knew he was finally being honest—with himself, and her.

'What are you saying?'

'That I love you,' he said now, no hesitation, no holds barred. 'And that you love me.' He frowned quickly. 'Or you did. It was wrong of me to question that, wrong of me to try to make you think that you didn't know your own heart. Not when you were wise enough to perceive what I refused to accept.'

He reached for her hands then, but took them slowly, carefully, giving her time to pull free if she didn't welcome the touch. She stayed right there, close to him, engulfed by him, comforted beyond words by what he was saying.

'It's the last thing I expected to happen, when I suggested this marriage. But in you, my darling, I found my other half. In you, I found my soul, my completion, my everything. And I will walk through the fires of hell before I let anything come between us. I will love you with all that I am, for all time, if you will come home to me.'

'Home,' she whispered, on an uneven sigh. Because 'home' had become his penthouse almost as soon as she'd moved in.

'I never want to stand in your way,' he said. 'I know you have big dreams, and I want to be by your side as you fulfil them. We can live anywhere, do anything. I just want you in my life, as my wife. My real wife, in so much more than name.'

She let out a sob, but, this time, of complete, exhaustive happiness and relief. She nodded quickly, wrapping her arms around his waist and standing on the tips of her toes, hugging him so his warmth and strength could soak into her. 'I love you,' she whispered, glancing up at him.

'I know.' He smiled then, a bright smile that told her so much. Because he'd grappled with this. With letting someone love him, with accepting that love, and letting it become a part of him, and now, finally, he got it. He was right there with her. They were unified in how much they loved, how much they needed each other, and they always would be.

* * *

Much, much later, when they were curled together in Amelia's small hotel bed, Massimiliano's fingers found her ring. 'I've been thinking about this,' he said, so she glanced down at the fake diamond. 'Oh?'

'You asked me to have a replica made, so I did.'

She nodded once.

'But it's not cut glass, darling. It's real diamond, real gold.'

She gasped. 'Massimiliano, I have been wearing this thing around as if…as if it didn't matter if it got lost or taken…'

'It's just a ring,' he reminded her. 'But my point is that it's real. That it's been real all along. Just like us.'

Her heart turned over in her chest and she blinked up at him through watery eyes. 'I believe I told you that, some time ago.'

'And you'll have the rest of our lives to hear me tell you that you were right.'

'The rest of our lives sounds pretty good, you know.'

'It sounds like heaven.' And he kissed her with all the love in his heart and the hope of their future. He kissed her like a man who had found his way home, to his love, his life, his wife, and never planned on letting her go.

And he didn't. Not for all the years of the rest of their lives, which were long, happy and blessed, in total, with four children—a son, a daughter, and twin sons to follow. In due course, Amelia's career aspirations took a slight twist. Rather than working as a doctor, she managed their foundation, which was exclusively for the funding of medical treatments and research. Her work was tireless and rewarding. The same could be said of parenting.

Marriage, though, was effortless. For all she'd heard about 'ups and downs', with Massimiliano, it was one perfect day after the next, one sensual night after another, so that her heart was for ever and always bursting at the seams, just as she deserved. Just as they both did.

* * * * *

Did Wedding Night Ultimatum *leave you wanting more? Then you're certain to love these other steamy stories from Clare Connelly!*

Twins for His Majesty
Billion-Dollar Dating Deception
Tycoon's Terms of Engagement
Blackmail to White Veil
Greek's Ring of Redemption

Available now!